Lock Down Publications and Ca$h
Presents

I0637481

CITY OF SMOKE 3

THE FALL OF MO MONEY

A Novel By
MOLOTTI

Lock Down Publications
P.O. Box 944
Stockbridge, GA 30281
www.lockdownpublications.com

Like our page on Facebook: Lock Down Publications
www.facebook.com/lockdownpublications.ldp

Stay Connected with Us!

Text **LOCKDOWN** to 22828 to stay up-to-date with new releases, sneak peaks, contests and more...

Like our page on Facebook:
Lock Down Publications

Join Lock Down Publications/The New Era Reading Group

Visit our website:
www.lockdownpublications.com

Follow us on Instagram:
Lock Down Publications

Email Us: We want to hear from you!

DEDICATION

All praises go to Allah and honors go to LDP CEO Ca$h and all of my fans. I value and appreciate all the support. Thanks. I wanna thank my mother Nikola Williams for the immense amount of support and love, I love you.

I wanna thank my cousin Nutso, who is also like my brother. I love you cuz, you been my hype man thru this whole journey, we stayed up till 3-4 in the morning reading manuscripts and your opinion means everything to me. Thanks cuz, I love the fuck outta you. When I win you win and that's why you push me so hard. I appreciate that.

Thanks to all my supporters. I love y'all. I got more heat coming soon

Chapter 1
Still In the Hundreds

Hot Rod walked out of Cook County Jail and stretched his lean body while inhaling the fresh summer air. He had spent the last five years of his life in the county fighting the murder of his best friend, which his twin brother, Bang, had committed. Hot Rod looked around and smiled when he seen a young girl with long hair running his way.

"Hey Daddy!" She shouted jumping into his arms.

Hot Rod spent most of his bid working out, so he easily lifted his daughter in the air. He felt nothing but joy as he looked into her eyes, which were a deep red. They were the same color as his, something that ran in their blood. He sat Mekiyah down just as a beautiful brown skinned woman strutted his way in a catsuit and a pair of Chanel heels.

"What's up, bae?" he asked her before hugging her tightly and giving her a juicy kiss.

"Hey, baby. Welcome home," the woman replied with tears welling up in her eyes. She was his daughter's mother, Kailyn, also the rapper known as Kayy Killa.

"Where Bang at?" Hot Rod asked expecting for his twin to be front and center.

"I don't know," Kailyn shrugged. "Somewhere running these streets."

"Do he know I'm home?"

"I didn't tell him, so if you haven't told him, then no."

"Good," Hot Rod said with a smile. "Let's go home. Tonight is our night and tomorrow I'ma make my presence be felt by everybody," he told Kailyn, following her to her car.

Unbeknownst to her or anyone else, he had big plans, and he was already ready to put the wheels in motion.

***

Bang sat in the passenger's seat of Mo Money's SRT Dodge Charger. His red pupils were dilated, due to the black Louie V X-Pill that they both were off.

"On Stone, Moe, let's go fuck somebody up!" Bang gruffed to Mo Money who was driving aimlessly through The 100's.

"Be cool, Law," Mo Money replied holding a hand up. "I'm waiting on a mufucka to drop this lo so we can pull up," he replied with a smile. His eyes darted to every one of his mirrors while he cruised. He was watching for Twelve, familiar cars or to make sure they weren't being followed.

"Who?"

"Don't trip," Mo Money replied once again flashing his signature grin. "Didn't I tell you that I had a surprise for you?"

"Yeah, but you know I don't like surprises."

"Whatever nigga, roll up," Mo Money said grabbing a pack of Backwoods from the side of his door and tossing it to Bang. After another thirty minutes of driving, he pulled into the driveway of some house in Ford Heights.

"Who crib is this?" Bang asked

"Just be on point and ready to blow," Mo Money replied, getting out the car.

Bang followed him to the front door and waited anxiously as he rang the doorbell. When the front door swung open, Bang's eyes lit up like a light. He was staring at Nell, the man who murdered his younger sister. He already had his .45 in his hand. He didn't hesitate to shoot Nell in his chest, knocking him backwards back into the house. Mo Maney jetted into the home and disappeared into the back.

"You been hiding for a long ass time," Bang told Nell with a broad smile on his face. "It's been five years since you killed lil sis. I been waiting on this moment," he said to Nell who laid on the soft carpet, holding his chest and gasping for air. The last time Nell had seen the young, red eyed devil, he was younger with shoulder length dreads. Now, he was bigger with long locks that hung almost to the middle of his back and tattoos covering his dark brown skin. Bang quickly scanned the room. The home seemed to be empty. He put the barrel of his Glock to Nell's forehead and repeatedly pulled the trigger. He smiled as he watched his brains splatter everywhere.

"You done?" Mo Money asked coming from the back of the home carrying two black duffle bags.

"Hold on," Bang replied before emptying the rest of his clip in Nell's face and neck. "We gone," he said, rushing out of the house.

"I told you I had you bro. It just took me a lil minute to get his location but I been had this cake baking for a while now," Mo Money explained after they hopped in the car and pulled off.

Bang sat there quietly looking out of his window. He was thinking about his sister, Mekiyah. He could sleep better now knowing that he avenged her death, and she was now resting in peace. "Thanks bro," he replied sincerely.

"You look out for me; I look out for you. That's what homies do," Mo Money replied and Bang shot him a funny look.

"Yeah, that's what homies do," he finally said before leaning back in his seat.

"Daddy, wake up!" Bang's five-year-old son Lil Blow yelled jumping onto his bed, awakening him from a deep slumber.

"What's up, lil dude?" Bang asked groggily.

"Somebody here for you."

"Who?" Bang asked looking Lil Blow in his red eyes.

"I don't know." Lil Blow shrugged his little shoulders. "He look like you, but mommy said he wasn't my daddy," he explained.

Bang was confused. He reached under his pillow and grabbed his Glock. "Stay right here," he told his son before leaving the room.

Bang entered the living room of the small home he shared with his son's mother, Alicia, to see Hot Rod standing there with a small smirk on his face. "When you get out?" He asked cracking a slight smile.

"Damn, I can't get a hug? A what's up bro? None of that good shit. Not even a welcome home?" Hot Rod asked.

Bang closed the space between them and gave him a tight hug. He really did miss him. This was the first time they'd seen each other since Hot Rod got locked up a little over five years ago.

"I'm happy you finally out that jam, bro. Welcome home," he told his brother. They were identical twins and before Hot Rod's arrest, they had almost identical body and facial structures. The only way you could tell which was which because Hot Rod was a shade lighter. Now, they were still around the same height about 6'1. They both had long dreads that hung down to the middle of their backs but now Hot Rod had way more muscle and bulk than his twin.

"Why didn't you let me know you was coming home? I could have been prepared for you. I got some paper for you, doe."

"I wanted to surprise you," Hot Rod told him, plopping down on Bang's red leather sofa.

"So, what you on now that you back out?" Bang asked, plucking a half-smoked wood out of the glass ashtray that sat on his coffee table and lighting it up. He knew that his brother was a hustler, and he was sure he planned on running it up.

"Bae, Mo Money on the phone," Alicia called from the bedroom before bringing Bang his phone.

"What's the demo, Law?" Bang asked grabbing the phone from her, admiring her thick body as she left the room. Give me a lil minute bro I'm kinda in the middle of something right now," he said into the phone after a few moments of listening. "All well, I'ma hit yo' line when I'm ready," he said before hanging up and tossing his phone on the couch. He caught his brother looking at him with a look of disgust on his face.

"What?" he asked.

"You still fuckin with that snake ass nigga?" Hot Rod asked with a frown.

"Yeah, we make good money together and he was the one who helped me get Nell out the way."

"Y'all smoked Nell?" Hot Rod asked surprised.

"I smoked Nell," Bang clarified. "But he called the play."

Hot Rod nodded. He didn't like Mo Money because he felt like he was the reason why their younger sister had gotten murdered, but he respected the fact that he assisted Bang in getting his get back. That still didn't make him like him, doe.

"How many blicks you got in here?" Hot Rod asked.

"A few, why?" Bang asked raising an eyebrow.

"I need one."

"For what?"

"Protection, dumbass. What else would I need a gun for?"

Bang chuckled and got up to head to his bedroom. He didn't want to get rid of any of his guns and since Hot Rod was fresh out, he didn't want to put a gun in his hands but he returned to the living room holding a Glock 19.

"This bitch ain't dirty, is it?" Hot Rod asked, grabbing the gun. It came out sounding as if he was kidding but he was dead serious. He knew firsthand how careless his brother was and he had already been a victim of something his twin did.

Bang smacked his lips. "Give me my shit back," he said, holding his hand out.

"I'm just fuckin with you lil bro," Hot Rod told him laughing. He stood up and put the gun on his waistline. "I got a few moves I need to make. I would tell you to keep the squares out yo' circle but you just can't get it right when it comes to whom you surround yo'self with. Just try to be safe," he told Bang preparing to leave.

"Yeah, you too, bro. I love you."

"Love you too," Hot Rod replied giving him a brotherly hug before leaving.

When Hot Rod left Bang's home, he drove to the 100's to pay one of his old cellies a visit. He turned his car on 104th Street and entered the parking lot to a big building. Once at the end of the parking lot, he parked, hopped out of his car and began to approach one of the balconies where a crowd of men stood not too far from.

"What's up?" A short brown skinned guy with deep waves, who looked like he was no older than 20 years old asked him.

"What up?" He replied.

"What you need?" The guy asked but Hot Rod ignored him as he continued to make his way toward the balcony.

"Aye, you don't hear me talking to you?" The little guy snapped making his way towards Hot Rod like he was going to do something to him.

Hot Rod continued to ignore him. He pulled out his phone and made a call. "I'm outside," he said to whoever he called and hung up. That's when he noticed the crowd of men mugging him. "What?" He asked the little guy returning his mug.

"We getting money out here, bro. You either bout to buy some drugs or move the fuck around. Ain't no standing around out here," the guy explained as Reesie came out of the apartment and hopped over the Balcony.

"What's the word, Solid?" Hot Rod asked him with a wide smile.

Reesie was a skinny brown skinned guy with long dreads that he had braided up. He had on a bussdown Cartier wristwatch as well as a bussdown Cuban link chain with an iced out 4X pendant swinging from it. He smiled showing his gap.

"When you get out?" He asked, dropping a gang sign with Hot Rod. When the other guys saw how he was carrying Hot Rod, they fell back.

"Yesterday," Hot Rod replied, following Reesie inside the building.

***

Life had been very good to Nutso as of lately. He was almost fully recovered from the bullets he took a few months ago. He was able to walk and run now and not only that, but he was gaining his strength and his weight back. His pockets were also doing much better due to the fact that he had split ways with his older cousin, Mo Money, who had robbed him and a few of his men the same night he had gotten shot up. To add insult to injury, Mo Money came to see him while he was on his deathbed. Nutso knew that the only reason why he robbed him was because he needed the money for his daughter's ransom, and he could've forgiven him for that but while he was on his deathbed, he confessed to him that it was him who had murdered his daughter's mother Precious. After hearing that, Mo Money pulled the plug to the machine that he thought was keeping him alive. Luckily, the machine that he unplugged was only the one that was monitoring Nut's heartrate. Nutso was devastated that his blood cousin, his best friend, had tried to take him out. Now, it was smoke.

"It's dry as hell out here," Nutso complained to his right-hand man, Binky.

"Hell yeah, I thought we was gon' catch something out here," Binky replied dryly gazing out his window hoping he saw a familiar face or car. He was a young nigga with brown skin, low cut wavy hair and a few tatts on his face. He was the definition of a demon. All he did was catch bodies and when he went too long without shooting his gun, it would have him in a bad mood. The two of them were riding through the few blocks that Mo Money were known to still frequent trying to see if they could catch him or one of the niggas who were riding with him. The thing with that was that the beef between them and Mo Money was personal and a few of the people who ran with him were still loyal to Nutso and would never bring any harm to him. He couldn't just ride through killing any and everybody. It was a complicated situation.

"This pussy ass nigga be hiding!" Nutso huffed turning his car up 104th and Rhodes. "Fuck it. Since we can't catch Money bitch ass, let's go see if we can catch Reesie or one of them hoe ass foes," he told Binky as he headed for Risky Road, the side of the hood that Reesie ran. Reesie was the man on Risky Road just like he was the man on D Block, the side of the hood that he ran. Mo Money wasn't good on either side of the hood, even doe he grew up on those same blocks.

When Nutso saw Reesie's Range Rover sitting on 104th and Corliss, he rode past and saw a group of men standing in front of the crib the Range was parked in front of one of the men caught his eye. "Was that Bang?" He asked Binky.

"On Stone, I was about to ask you the same thing," Binky replied.

Nutso doubled back around the block and when he saw that his eyes weren't deceiving him, he stopped his car in the middle of the block.

"Bang, what the fuck you doing over here?" He yelled out his window. He had his Glock 23 clutched in his hand, ready to start blowing. He peeped the surprise in Bang's face and didn't like when a frown formed on his face.

"Fuck you!" Hot Rod yelled causing him to quickly point his Glock out the window and start blowing. He really thought that Hot Rod was Bang. Hot Rod and Reesie, who was standing next to him, returned fire. Binky jumped out the car and was shooting over the hood.

"Hop in!" Nutso urged him when a couple more guns went off. Nutso peeled off angrily. "That snake ass nigga!" He growled thinking about Bang being posted with the Foes.

The Black Stones and the Corner Hustlers were in a bloody war that took a lot from Nutso. He was mad because he really fucked with Bang but after seeing him with Reesie all that shit was dead. He knew how the game went so he wasn't tripping. He simply added Bang to the already long list of niggas he was going to step on. He started wondering how was Bang fucking with Reesie and Mo Money when they hated each other? It was some real backdoor shit going on and he knew for a fact that bodies would be piling up real soon. Until then, he planned on playing more offense than defense.

***

Mo Money laid in his bed with his son, King sleeping on his chest and his daughter, Paradise was snuggled between him and King's mother, Deja. It was the crack of dawn and he was up ready to start his day. He got up as quiet as he possibly could and laid King next to his sister before going into the living room. He grabbed a pre-rolled Backwood stuffed with exotic weed and flamed it up before peeking out of the living room's window. He was far from a coward. He wasn't even being paranoid. He just knew that it was a lot of niggas who wanted him dead and he'd rather be safe than sorry.

He used to be one of the faces of a gang of young niggas that had the 100's on lock but that was when Risky Road and D Block, the Moes and the Foes were all together. That was in his younger days, even though those days were merely years ago. He was still young but a lot had changed over the years. His whole team were either dead or opps now. He was once the plug but now he robbed and killed for the drugs he sold. He was once looked at as a respectable hustler but now the streets saw him as a snake. The backdoor was always open when he was around. Nobody trusted him. He didn't even trust himself. He was a loner and surprisingly that didn't bother him at all. He had lost his daughter once and that drove him insane. The situation knocked the wind out of him and turned him into the monster he now was. The vibrating of his phone snapped him out of his thoughts.

"What's the word?" he answered in a hushed tone.

"Can you come over?" A soft voice asked him.

"Yeah, I'm on my way," he told the woman before hanging up on her. He tiptoed back into his bedroom and grabbed his Glock 21 off his nightstand.

"Where are you going this early?" Deja asked barely awake.

"I gotta go handle some business."

"Be safe. I love you," she replied, knowing that that usually meant he had some trouble to get into.

"I love you too, bae," he told her bending over to kiss her forehead before leaving.

Mo Money drove to the east side of the city. He made it to 69th and Clyde and cruised up the block. Once he rode through the block and was on his way back around, he made a call and told the person to, "Come outside." Then, he parked, got out the car and headed for a house towards the end of the block where a tall, petite, peanut butter colored woman stood on the porch.

"Boy come on!" The woman urged him. He put some pep in his step and followed her inside her home. Before he could close the door; she turned around and gave him a passionate kiss.

"Ugh, you looking bad!" She frowned looking at his nappy dreads and the dark bags under his eyes.

"That's what you called me over here for?" He asked shooting her a funny look.

"No, I miss you—"

"Get the fuck outta here!" He snapped waving her off, hurting her feelings. At one point, she had his brain. She was his Kryptonite and her word was gold to him but that was before. His heart beat to a different rhythm now.

"Baby Dre, it's been months and you still acting weird. What's wrong with you?"

"YOU," Mo Money said to his first and only true love, Ashley. He was staring in her big, round, brown eyes. She was used to him chasing her not him neglecting her like he'd been doing lately. "You supposed to be my R-O-D but I don't see it. You don't love me like you say you do," he said, folding his arms across his chest.

"I am your R-O-D."

"On Stone, you ain't been acting like it. You need to prove that shit," he said. Ashley closed the space between them and asked, "How?" before gently kissing his lips. He didn't respond. He just started kissing her. It didn't take too many kisses for him to get her out of her clothes. He laid her down on her soft, red carpet that covered her living room floor. She quickly spread her long legs, anxious to feel him inside of her. He quickly undressed so he could give her what she wanted.

"I love youuu," Ashley purred as he thrusted in and out of her wet pussy. No man on earth knew her body like he did.

"I love you more," he whispered in her ear before nibbling her earlobe.

After twenty minutes of making love, he wanted to fuck so he flipped her over.

"How much do you love me? "He asked smacking her ass while he hammered in and out of her.

"A lottt," she whined.

"And what if a lot ain't enough?" He asked fucking her even harder. She was enjoying the sex so much that she couldn't answer. "Ashley what if a lot ain't enough for me?" He asked grabbing the back of her neck and giving it a light squeeze.

"Then, I'll love you more," she squealed before letting out a loud moan before she had an orgasm and started squirting.

Mo Money wasn't done with her. He turned her over, laid her down on the carpet and climbed on top of her, "You gotta prove that shit," he said sliding his dick back inside her.

"Okkkay, just tell me how," Ashley replied barely able to speak.

Mo Money stopped mid-stroke. "Get dressed so we can talk about it," he told her with a devilish grin.

"We're not talking about shit until you're done," she replied wrapping her long legs around his waist. He had a master plan and he needed her assistance. He planned on giving her the best dick she had in a long time to ensure her cooperation.

"I love you girl," he told her before going back to work.

***

Hot Rod sat in Prince's trap watching B Moe bag up brick into pieces. The scene brought back so many memories and the sight of the brick of coke had him anxious to get his hands dirty. Prince and B Moe were a major part of his support system while he was away. He looked at B Moe like a big brother and Prince was like a father figure to him. They were his family.

"You ready to run yo' bag to the roof?" Prince asked Hot Rod even though he already knew the answer. Prince was in his early forties with short dreads and a goatee. He had light skin and a deep voice that commanded attention when he spoke.

"Hell yeah," Hot Rod replied with a smile.

"I got a brick of soft for you. This one on the house. Consider it a welcome home gift. I'ma need thirty-five grand for the next one."

"Damn, why so much?"

"It ain't 2010 no more lil nigga. Its fucked up out here. Niggas paying one seventy-five for an eight ball and 1200 for a zip," Prince replied.

"I got a spot in the 100's that I'ma set up," Hot Rod was saying just as somebody knocked on the front door. B Moe opened the door and a short, light skinned guy with a low cut and a big nose entered the trap.

"Damn man, I been calling yo' phone since this morning! You ignoring my calls like I'm yo' bitch or something," The guy snapped at B Moe.

"I texted you and told you that I was gon' send somebody yo way," B Moe replied unmoved by the guy's attitude.

"I ain't yo' bitch nigga! Don't text me. Call me and talk to me like a man," The guy shot back causing both Prince and Hot Rod to erupt in laughter.

"Who the fuck is fam?" He asked mugging Hot Rod.

"Slow down, lil bro," Prince said holding up a hand." I want you to meet my little brother, Hot Rod. He's the guy that I've been telling you about," Prince told the guy before turning to Hot Rod. "This is B Moe's younger cousin, Powder. This lil nigga reminds me of you when you was younger," he said with a smile.

"What's up folks?" Powder asked Hot Rod, extending his hand for a shake.

"I'm one of the Moes bro," Hot Rod replied with a nod. "I got a few moves to make. I'ma holla at y'all later," he said leaving Powder hanging.

"It's good to see you bro. I'm glad you back," B Moe told him, giving him a brotherly hug.

"You already know, Law," Hot Rod replied.

"Keep yo' head up lil bro," Prince told him as he left the trap.

"I don't like dude goofy ass," Powder said with a frown after Hot Rod was gone.

"You don't even know him," B Moe replied waving him off.

"Nigga acted like he was too good to shake my hand. That's some girl shit."

"He just got out from doing a bid. He don't know you. He still got that County mentality," Prince explained.

"Ain't no excuses for acting like a bitch. If the nigga a bitch, he a bitch. You say I don't know the nigga but from what I do know, I know he a bitch," Powder said, irritating B Moe. He was 17 years old but sometimes acted like a 14-year-old. One thing about him was that he was a hustler. That's why B Moe took him under his wing.

"Here," B Moe said passing him two ounces of crack. "Get the fuck on somewhere," he told him tired of hearing his mouth already.

"I see that birds of a feather really flock together," Powder quipped before leaving the trap.

"In so many words he just called me a bitch, didn't he?" B Moe asked Prince who couldn't help but burst out laughing.

After leaving Prince's trap, Hot Rod went straight to one of Reesie's spots on Risky Road.

"What's up, gang?" Ressie asked Hot Rod as he entered the backroom of the home where Reesie was watching a few of his shorties weigh and bag up exotic weed.

"What the crack be doing out here?" Hot Rod asked flaming up a wood.

"I get that shit off when I come across it, but the dog food is what's really bringing the paper in. That plus the exotic and X pills."

"I got a connect on some good ass crack," Hot Rod told him as his homie Racks walked into the room.

"I'm good, bro," Reesie replied before taking a gulp from the double cup he was holding.

"So, what if I wanted to open up shop out here? Would you be cool with that?"

"You don't even know the area or any clucks in the area."

"That's where you and yo' peoples come in at. You could put me a lil team together just to get shit off the ground while I learn the land," Hot Rod said causing Racks to snort.

"How would that benefit us?" Racks asked.

"I don't know how much the workers gon' make that's something you gotta holla at Foe about," Hot Rod replied offending him.

"Do I look like a mufucking worker?"

"You don't look like Reesie so I don't know why you in my mufuckin' business," Hot Rod snapped.

The look on Racks face made Reesie crack a smile. He loved drama and he knew by his facial expression that Racks was ready to take it there with Hot Rod.

"Leave that shit alone man," he told them both.

"Look you can check thirty-five percent of whatever the trap bring in until I get familiar with everything and then you get fifteen percent of whatever I bring in," Hot Rod proposed.

"On the Foe, that sound good." Reesie nodded before taking another sip from his Styrofoam cup.

"You won't have to spend a dime so you basically making money free money. You can't lose."

"So, how much work you got?" Racks asked in a manner that pissed Hot Rod off.

Hot Rod sighed. "Bro why the fuck you keep talking to me?" He asked.

"Cause I can. You got a problem with it?" Racks shot back dropping his hand near his waist where his Glock rested.

"Fall back, Foe," Reesie told his enforcer. "Shit, how much work do you got? I want to know too," he asked Hot rod who was eying Racks with a sinister grin on his face. He remembered the stories that Reesie would tell him about Racks. He heard that he was a real stepper but that didn't mean shit to him. He noticed that Racks didn't think he could get smoked like every other tough guy running around.

"Right now, I got a brick and a half," Hot Rod replied.

"I got somewhere where you can open up at. Just give me a couple days to set everything up for you and it's a go."

"Bet," Hot Rod said preparing to leave. "You want to meet me outside or something?" He asked Racks, who was mean mugging him.

"We gone bump heads," Racks promised staring a hole through Hot Rod's back as he walked out.

Chapter 2

The Enemy of my Enemy

Arab walked out of his father's funeral with mixed emotions. He didn't have a great relationship with his father but they had been communicating and trying to patch things up before he got killed.

"You good bro?" Flock asked him, putting her hand on his shoulder. She had her long dreads fishtailed and the Burberry button up she had on covered up her tatted up, light brown skin. She was a dyke but that only fooled the ones who didn't know her resume. She was as dangerous as any man, and she was Arab's right-hand man.

"Yeah, I'm straight," Arab mumbled looking up to see Nutso approaching him, dressed in a navy blue Louis Vuitton suit. For a gangsta, he knew how to dress and make himself appear to be a successful businessman or something.

"What's the demo, Law? How you holding up?" He asked Arab. They shook up Black Stone then embraced in a brotherly hug.

"I'm well, Law. What's up with you?"

"I had to come show some love. It fucked me up when I found out that Nell was your pops. How the fuck y'all keep that a secret for so long?"

"We wasn't that close. We was when I was younger, but you know how that shit go."

"Them niggas bogus as hell man," Nutso said walking him and Flock to their car. When they got to the car, he flamed up a wood.

"Yeah, whoever did that shit made sure they ran thru the crib and emptied his shit after they fucked him up," Arab replied looking at the ground.

"So, it was a home invasion murder?" He asked passing Flock the wood he had just lit. He knew all the answers to his questions. He just wanted to pick Arab's brain and see what he knew.

"Yeah, that's what they say."

"Ain't it weird doe? That a mufucka overkilled him? You know how a home invasion goes. Even if you have to pop a mufucka, you not gon' overkill him, right or wrong? Even if a mufucka saw yo' face you wouldn't have emptied the clip in his face."

"He right doe," Flock agreed. Arab didn't speak. He stood there impassively while listening to Nut.

"That shit was more than just a home invasion," Nutso said. "Somebody he knew had to be the one who got his location and he brung along somebody who wanted yo' pops dead, badly."

"So, what you getting at?" Arab asked

"Mo Money and Bang," Nutso replied.

Arab digested his theory and in a way it did add up. He knew that Mo Money had basically given up on hustling and was now robbing all his clientele and old associates. He knew about the history between his father and Bang. Nell told him that it was Bang who murdered his younger brother and he also let him know that he retaliated by killing Bang's younger sister. For that reason alone, Arab decided not to kill Bang. He felt like losing his baby sister was enough, but now to hear Nut's theory had him seeing red.

"Think about that doe Moe and Stay dangerous," Nutso told him before shaking up with him and Flock before casually strolling off to his car.

Arab's mind raced as he dwelled on his words. He hadn't said a word to Flock as they drove through the city. Everything Nutso had said made sense. Mo Money and Bang were very close and lately Mo Money had been acting strange. He could've set it up and had Bang kill his pops while he emptied his home of all the drugs and money he could find. He was cutthroat like that. If he robbed Nutso, then he was sure he would rob anyone else. He knew how close they were so now he couldn't put shit past Mo Money.

"You think that shit Nut said was valid?" He asked Flock breaking the silence.

"If anybody would know, it would be Nutso."

"On Stone," Arab said nodding in agreement. "But at the end of the day him and Mo Money cousins. Why would he just throw him under the bus like that?"

"Dude tried to kill him. What do you expect?"

"That's true but I figured that he would want to do whatever he was gon' do to him himself instead of having somebody else do it."

"Maybe he want him dead but he can't do it himself so he planting seeds in yo' head to have you do it for him."

"You think so?" Arab asked.

Flock was silent for a moment. She was tryna make sure she gave her boy the best advice she possibly could.

"Look, you don't know for sure if that shit true or not," she paused to hit the smoldering wood she was holding before continuing. "But I say you do yo' homework and at the same time, work Nut and see what info you can get out of him. If shit point at Mo Money and Bang, then handle yo' business and I got yo' back the whole way," Flock said and she meant every word. Mo Money and Bang were both good peoples but Arab was family and if she had to choose, she would pick him every single time.

Arab cherished the friendship they had. Ever since his homie Barn Barn traded on him, he didn't let anyone close to him, but Flock was cut different. They were alike in so many ways and he trusted her with his life.

"Say less," Arab said formulating a plan in his mind as they rode around smoking.

***

"So, you sure it's a go?" Bang asked Mo Money. They were in a rental car riding around smoking exotic while they plotted their next lick.

"On Stone, I been in shorty ear about that shit and it took a while but she finally agreed to set it up for me," Mo Money replied.

"So, when you thinking about making it happen?"

"Just be patient. We can't rush this one."

"What's up with that other lick you say you had lined up for us?"

"It's a greenlight on that tonight. You must be fucked up, Law?" Mo Money asked choking on exotic smoke.

"Hell naw, what made you say that?" Bang asked with a chuckle.

"Cause you on my ass like you down to yo' last dollars."

"Naw," Bang shook his head. "You know I be sitting on my shit," he added as Mo Money pulled into a McDonald's parking lot. They walked in and saw Arab and Flock standing in line.

"What's the demo, Law?" Mo Money asked Arab, walking up behind him.

"What up?" Arab replied dryly. He wasn't feeling him at the moment.

"What y'all all dressed up for?" Mo Money asked, looking at the casual Burberry outfits that they both wore. He didn't seem to pick up on Arab's vibe.

"Today was my pops funeral."

"Damn, I'm sorry to hear that, beloved."

"I'm surprised that you didn't show up. I heard that you and my pops did a lil business together."

"Who was your pops?"

"Nell," Arab said causing Mo Money to tense up. He peeked over at Bang and caught him shooting him a weird look.

"Get the fuck outta here," Mo Money replied not able to mask his surprise.

"On Stone." Arab nodded. "Somebody ran in his crib and did him dirty. I know you heard about that shit."

"I heard about him getting killed but I haven't heard no details about what happened," Mo Money lied quickly.

"Damn, I was hoping you could've pointed me in the right direction as far as where that shit came from."

"Naw, I don't know too much of nothing but now that I know that Nell was yo' pops, I'ma most definitely do some digging."

"What's up bro? You cool?" Arab asked Bang who was staring at him.

"Hell yeah, how about you?" Bang replied.

"I'm well," Arab replied. He wanted to shoot him all in his face and little did he know, Bang was feeling the exact same way about him.

"We got some moves to makes so we bout to slide—"

"Y'all ain't even order no food," Flock said cutting Mo Money off. She was getting bad vibes from both of them and she didn't like the look in Bang's eyes. Her hand subtly slid near her waist.

"We ain't come in to order shit," Mo Money said flashing a smile. "We saw the whip outside, so we popped in to see what was up with y'all. Y'all keep y'all head up and stay dangerous," he said making his way out the restaurant.

"Damn. On Stone, that nigga Nutso probably was telling the truth," Flock said to Arab once they were gone.

"Why you say that?" Arab asked grabbing her food.

"First off nigga, Mo Money said they came in because they saw yo' car but we in a rental, gang. Then, after you let him know that Nell was yo' pops, that red eyed mufucka Bang wouldn't stop mugging you. Them niggas just giving off backdoor vibes."

You right." Arab nodded. "Mo Money was just acting weird as hell. He couldn't even look me in my eyes. I'ma do some homework but to be honest I'm ready to clap one of they ass," he told Flock who was taking a big bite out of her Big Mac.

"Let's do it," she replied with a smile as he pulled off.

***

Reesie let Hot Rod open up shop in a trap he had on 105th and Corliss. Two weeks after he did a pass out, he was seeing nonstop traffic. The trap stayed open twenty-four, seven and he had big bags of good crack, so the hypes were loving it. He had a team of Reesie's men working the trap but after constant harassment from B Moe, he gave in and let Powder oversee the trap. At first, Powder didn't want to hustle out of his spot but after B Moe explained what his job as an overseer was, he gladly accepted feeling like he was getting paid to babysit a few grown ass men.

"What's up, lil bro?" Hot Rod asked Powder entering the kitchen of the trap.

The two didn't really speak much but that was because they never had the chance to build and really get to know one another.

"What's the word?" Powder replied, placing chunks of crack on a small scale.

"What this bitch been doing?"

"Yesterday we checked a few thousand. Them niggas lazy as hell, doe."

"What they do?"

"This bitch will be doing way better if I was doing everything. Them niggas don't know how to cook up. They act like they don't know how to bag up. All them niggas do is play the fuckin X-Box all day. Sometimes, they don't even answer the door," he informed Hot Rod who was visibly angered by the news.

Hot Rod stomped off to the front room where a few of the Foes were playing NBA 2K. Due to the bottles that they were drinking, the many woods that they had in rotation and the group of women the guys were entertaining, it looked like they were having a kickback.

"What the fuck is y'all doing?" Hot Rod asked standing in front of the TV.

"We cooling, what's up?" A tall, chubby, light skinned Foe asked.

"You niggas supposed to be in here working, not cooling. This a trap, not Dave and Buster's!" He snapped.

"We waiting on Powder to finish bagging up."

"He not here to be bagging up. That's what y'all here for!" Hot Rod said pointing a finger in the guy's face. "What, you don't know how to use a scale or something?"

"Why should we do it if he gon' do it?" The guy asked with a chuckle. He was trying to look like a somebody in front of the hoes. "This our shit. He gotta put in some work too," he said.

"This y'all shit?" Hot Rod asked walking up on the guy. It looked like he was about to give the wrong answer so he took off on him. He beat the man brutally while everybody else watched. Apparently, one of the older Foes didn't like what he was seeing so he got up and made his way to assist his homie. He didn't get far before Powder hit him in the back of the head with the butt of his gun. He then viciously pistol whipped him until he stopped moving.

"Anybody else got a problem or some more dumb shit to say?" Hot Rod asked after snatching the gun from Powder's hand and pointing it at the other three men in the room.

"Naw man," one guy said. He was scared shitless.

"If I hear about you niggas being in here on some lazy shit, sitting on y'all asses like this work gon' sell itself, I'ma fuck one of y'all up. He not here to work for y'all," he said pointing towards Powder. "Y'all work for him," he added as Reesie and Racks walked through the front door.

"Fuck is going on in here?" Racks asked upping his Glock at the sight of one of his guys laying bloody on the floor.

"We coming to an understanding," Hot Rod told him, still trying to catch his breath.

"What the fuck happened bro?" Reesie asked looking around the room.

"They was in this bitch tweaking. They don't cook up or bag up. They in this bitch partying instead of making money so when I addressed that shit, they tell me that this they shit and we not from out here—"

"Y'all not!" Racks stated, cutting Hot Rod off. Workers or not, he didn't like the way he had handled his homies. "This they hood and you bogus for carrying them like it's not. Nigga you a guest," he added.

"This MY hood," Reesie corrected him before turning to Hot Rod. "I didn't know Foe nem was in here moving like that. They told me this bitch was booming."

"It is but it could be doing better," Powder said causing both Reesie and Racks to look at him funny.

"Who the fuck is shorty?" Racks asked, screwing his face up.

"He with me," Hot Rod said.

"Let me know before you just bring a mufucka over here."

"Man, get yo' goofy ass outta here!" Hot Rod told him, waving him off. He was going to play it cool with him out of the respect he had for Reesie but Racks was asking for it.

Racks tightened the grip on the Glock he held. "I'm getting tired of this fake ass tough guy act you putting on. You ain't gangsta because you did a few years," he said with a sneer on his face. Him and Hot Rod were both muscular guys with bad attitudes. They were like a lion and a tiger ready to go at it to the death. Reesie stood there silently, watching while occasionally taking a sip from his double cup. He knew that Racks was a killer and he also knew that Hot Rod got like that too.

"What you think they stopped making killers when they made you?" Hot Rod asked Racks, mugging him.

"Leave that shit alone man," Reesie finally spoke up sensing that somebody was closed to getting smoked.

"On the Foe, you not gon' be able to keep saving this lame ass nigga," Racks complained.

"He not saving shit nigga. If you stop woofing and do you, then he wouldn't be able to save shit," Hot Rod retorted.

"Man get the fuck up!" Reesie told his two men who were still laying on the floor. "On the Foe, y'all making us look bad. I should have somebody clap y'all dumb asses," he told the men watching them get up and limp out the trap as fast as they could.

"Other than that, you well?" He asked Hot Rod before taking another sip from his double cup.

"Hell yeah, I was about to hit yo' line and see if you wanted to slide on them hoe niggas but something came up in the hood so I gotta shoot that way real quick and see what's up."

"Aight, I'ma send some more of the bros over here to fill in for them fuck up ass niggas."

"Naw," Hot Rod said shaking his head, cutting him off. "I'm cool, bro. I'm sure we won't have no more misunderstandings," he said looking at the remaining two men.

"Say less," Reesie replied before leading Racks, Hot Rod and Powder out of the trap. Just like that the Foes that were left in the trap kicked their hoes out, turned off the game and got into trap mode.

"You straight?" Hot Rod asked Powder as they climbed in his Volkswagen.

"Hell yeah," Powder nodded pulling out a Wood and unraveling it.

"Good looking too for that aid and assistance."

"It ain't shit, gang. B Moe and Prince say you family so that's what it is."

"Fasho, I don't like that hoe ass nigga, Racks," Hot Rod said frowning.

"Let's smoke him," Powder suggested making him laugh.

"It ain't that simple, bro. Reesie my homie and that's his right hand man. We got a lot going on right now and I'm not tryna let that fake tough ass nigga interfere with my bread."

"Fasho, just keep yo' eyes on that nigga. I would hate for him to beat you to the punch."

"Don't shit beat the cross but the double cross. I'm all over his ass," Hot Rod said and they shared a laugh.

This was their first time really rotating and the little situation had brung them closer. It was the start of a bond. They smoked the Wood and Hot Rod watched him head back into the trap before going his own way.

Hot Rod entered his home to see Kailyn and Alicia in the front room watching his daughter and nephew play together.

"Hey bae," Kailyn said to him.

"Nothing much," he replied bending over to give her a peck on the lips. "What y'all up to?" He asked, making his way toward the kitchen.

"Nothing. We probably about to take the kids to the movies or to SkyZone," Kailyn hollered as she watched him leave the kitchen and head for their bedroom.

He entered his bedroom and went straight for his closet. He dug around until he pulled out a dusty Adidas duffle bag. He went in the bag and pulled out a few bricks of money.

"What are you doing with all that money?" Kailyn asked, entering the room.

"I got some business to handle. Why? What's up? You need something?"

"No, I was just asking," she replied softly.

"Come here," he said patting the empty space on the bed next to him.

"You know I love you more than anything in this world right?" He asked and she nodded. "You sacrificed over five years of your life for me and I can't thank you enough for that. I can see it all in yo' eyes that you worried about something. I don't know what it is that you worried about but I know you're worried. Tell me what's on your mind."

"I just don't want to lose you again."

"Why do you think you're going to lose me?"

"I been having these crazy nightmares ever since you've been home. It doesn't make it any better that you've been running the streets all day and night, instead of being here at home with me and Mekiyah where you belong. The streets didn't do that time with you. We did," Kailyn said finally expressing the feelings that she'd been trying to hide from him.

"And I appreciate every single second you did with me but don't throw that in my face," Hot Rod replied sternly.

"I'm not throwing it in your face. I'm just letting you know that it's not fair for you to run in and out of our lives. If you're going to be here, STAY here, because I don't know if I could spend another five years by myself," Kailyn said before getting up and leaving the room.

Hot Rod sat there for a few minutes thinking about what she'd just said. She had every right to feel how she felt and he knew that. He stuffed two of the bricks of money in his backpack and left the house.

Chapter 3
Illusions

"Mo Money entered an apartment the had rented out on 92nd and King Drive.

"What y'all on?" He asked the trio that were in the front room smoking a wood and scrolling through their phones.

"What's the word, Sane?" One of the guys asked. He was shorty, husky, brown skinned with small dreads.

"Aye, Lil Dav, what I tell you about that Sane shit?" Mo Money snapped making him chuckle.

"I'm Sane Gang, bro. That's how I talk," he replied with a small smirk on his face. He was from Lavergne and Adams, a hood known as Sane Gang. He was a Mafia Insane Vice Lord, due to his hot temper and itchy trigger finger. He had to relocate from out west to the 100's with his cousin, Breezy, who was a Black Stone from Risky Road. That's how he met Mo Money.

"That nigga be blowing you, don't he?" Breezy asked speaking for the first time. He was a skinny, brown skinned guy who stood about 5'10. He had a sponged fro and dark eyes that seemed to watch everything. He was riding with Mo Money against Nutso and everybody else besides Reesie. He still had a lot of love for him.

Mo Money wasn't too much selling drugs anymore but he always kept his homies, Von D and Lil Rodney flooded with whatever work he came up on and they would get that shit off and kick him out some of the profit. They had a good thing going and it worked for everyone involved. Lil Rodney was one of the lil Foes from Risky Road. Those three along with Von D and Bang were the only men Mo Money considered friends. Everyone else was food in his eyes.

"What the fuck y'all on in this bitch?" Mo Money asked.

"We was in traffic till dumb ass right here," Breezy nodded towards Lil Dav, "Blew a mufucka down on the Eway."

"I thought he was an opp," Lil Dav claimed with a smirk.

"What else been going on?"

"Shit really." Breezy shrugged. "Nut and Binky rode through earlier and they had a shootout with them."

"How much work you got left?" Mo Money asked Lil Rodney.

"That shit will be gone by the morning," he replied. He was the most cool, calm and collected out of the group. He loved making money, fucking hoes and buying clothes but he was also the type who went from zero to a hundred in a second if you rubbed him the wrong way. It didn't take much to make him put the work down and pick his gun up.

"All well, I got a brick at the crib. One of y'all can pick it up from me later. Where my bread at?" Mo Money asked and Lil Rodney got up from the couch and went into the backroom of the apartment. He returned with a paper bag that Mo Money knew for sure was filled with money.

"Do I gotta count this shit?" he asked.

"Damn Sane, what you think we gon' get down on you?" Lil Dav asked.

"I see I'ma have to fuck you up," Mo Money threatened, making everybody erupt in laughter. Lil Dav loved fucking with him.

"Damn, Lord, that's how you feeling?"

"I'm tryna talk business and yo' goofy ass want to keep playing."

"Aight, what's the demo, beloved?" Lil Dav asked, doing his best Black Stone impersonation.

"I just bought some new blicks and a new hot car. Let's go catch something," Mo Money said flashing his signature smile. He knew that that would end the joking.

"Man, you shoulda been said that!" Lil Dav said, making his way out of the apartment followed by Breezy.

"Rodney, you stay here and get the rest of that work off," Mo Money said.

He needed somebody to focus on making some money. Plus, he knew it was a chance that they ran into the Foes and he didn't want to put him in an awkward position cause just like Breezy, Rodney still had love for all of his Risky Road homies, The Foes and Moes.

"Aight," Rodney said dropping a gang sign with Mo Money before he left. After sending a few shots at the BDs, Mo Money picked up the brick from his home and dropped Lil Dav and Breezy off at the trap before heading back home.

"Hey, stink," Deja greeted him as he entered his home.

"What's up baby?" He asked as he kicked off his Retro Jordans and plopped down on their black leather couch. "Come here," he told her, and she came and took a seat on his lap.

"What's up, daddy?" She asked flirtatiously.

"Ain't nothing up. I just been missing yo' fine ass. I been thinking about you all fucking day."

"And what were you thinking?"

"Well, first I was thinking about how much I was missing you. Then, I started thinking about how fine you is and when I started thinking about all yo' sexiness, my dick got hard as hell. I started thinking about all the nasty shit I was gon' do to you once I made it in," he said before kissing her on her neck. He knew that was her spot.

"Stop before you start something," she said with a giggle.

"That's what I'm tryna do," Mo Money replied sliding his hands in her boy shorts. Her eyes rolled to the back of her head as he rubbed her clit in a circular motion. He knew exactly how she liked to be touched. It didn't take long for his dick to rock up and when it did, Deja wasted no time in climbing from his lap, getting down on her knees and giving him some good top. That led to an hour long sex session that ended with them cuddled up in their big bed.

"So, what's up?" Mo Money asked Deja while staring at the ceiling.

"What's up with what?" She asked, confused by the question.

"You, how you feeling? What's on your mind?"

"Nothing really. I been having some crazy ass dreams lately."

"Tell me about them."

"They be crazy like everything be all bad for me and the kids and you be like this angel with big, black wings and you always tell me to 'Be strong' and that its always rain before the sunshine' but that don't even be the scary part. The scary part be that you be the one that's hurting everybody and you was fighting yourself not to hurt me and the kids," she explained.

Mo Money laid there contemplating his response. "It's just a dream. I'm not gon' hurt you," he assured her but instead of making her feel secure, he did the exact opposite, making her scoot away from him.

"What's wrong?" He asked looking at her with wide eyes.

"I'm not gon' hurt you. That's the same thing you tell me in my dreams right before you try to kill me," she told him before turning over and pulling the cover up to her neck.

The next morning, Mo Money was out early making his rounds. Everything was cool until he noticed a dark blue Nissan following him. He noticed that the driver of the Nissan was his younger cousin, Ralph. He stopped in front of the Nissan and hopped out of his car. "Ralph, why the fuck you following me? I almost shot that lil ass car up," he said loudly while approaching the car his cousin was in. When he got about ten feet from the car, the passenger, who was a young guy he didn't recognize, hopped out and started shooting a .357 at him.

"FUCK!" He gruffed turning around and bolting back to his car.

As he climbed in, Ralph started to ram the back of his car while his homie continued to shoot. Mo Money counted the shots and when he counted shot number six, he popped back out of his car with his Glock aimed at the Nissan. He didn't want to but he squeezed the trigger sending shots into the windshield trying to hit the passenger more so than his cousin. Ralph stomped on the brakes and reversed until he could turn down a side block and escape the barrage of bullets. Mo Money was fuming. He knew that nobody but Nutso had sent Ralph and he was disappointed that he would put him in harm's way like that.

Mo Money couldn't shake thinking about Ralph trying to get him as he rode around listening to G Herbo's 'I'm Rolling. He wasn't sure what he really wanted to do so he pulled out his phone and facetimed Nutso.

"What?" Nutso answered with a frown on his face.

"What's the demo, bloody?" Mo Money asked flashing a smile.

"You tell me. You the one calling my phone."

"You dumb as hell for sending Ralph at me, cuz. I shoulda popped his hoe ass."

"That wasn't my work, cuz," Nutso replied honestly. He was actually surprised to hear that Ralph had shot at him.

"Let's squash this petty ass beef and live our lives because I'm not tryna have none of my aunties crying, mad at me cause I done spanked one of they sons, you feel me?"

"You tried to kill me. I'm not leaving shit alone until you dead," Nutso replied and Mo Money could hear the seriousness in his voice.

"I was just playing with yo' soft ass. I knew that machine wasn't keeping you alive," Mo Money lied unable to contain his smile.

"Fuck outta here!" Nutso spat angrily.

"On Stone, since you feel that way, let's get this shit over with tonight. Where you at?"

"I'm on my block," Nutso replied cooly.

"On my kids, I'm 'bout to pull up," Mo Money said before hanging up the phone. He quickly drove home before making his way to D Block. "I'm out here," he said to Nutso after calling him back. He got out of his car and posted in the middle of 107th and Indiana, holding both Paradise and King in his arms. He watched as Nut, followed by a few of the Moes came out of one of the houses on the block and headed his way.

"You a dirty ass nigga!" Nutso said with a frown when he seen Mo Money standing there holding his kids. "Just when I think you at yo' lowest, you find a way to get lower. You think just because you brought the kids out you won't get yo' ass smoked?" He asked.

"I know I won't. At least not right here," Mo Money replied confidently flashing that friendly smile that hid his venomous fangs. "Now, let's talk, cuz. Tell yo' fans to fall back before I get mad."

Nut stared at him for a second before nodding indicating for his men to fall back. "What's up?" He asked with an attitude.

"I'm done with all this shit. I got my daughter back. I gave her a brother. I don't owe nobody no money. I'm ready to walk away while I still can," Mo Money said sincerely.

This wasn't his first time saying it so Nut halfway believed him. "Cuz, you tried to kill me, yo blood, yo right hand and you want me to just look past that shit?"

"Forgive and forget," Mo Money suggested with a smile.

"What about Reesie? He gone forgive and forget too?"

"I'ma handle him. I just gotta make sure I don't gotta worry about my lil cousin killing me."

"I never thought I had to worry about my big cousin killing me, but you tried," Nutso shot back with a hint of sadness in his tone.

"You killed Precious!" Mo Money said loudly, startling his children. "On Stone, you killed her and left me in the dark about that shit. You knew what I was going through and you ain't have the nuts to tell me that you was the reason why I was hurting. You took my daughter's mother from her," he said lowering his tone. He never admitted it to anyone but losing Precious took a toll on him. He really did love her and he regretted not being able to experience being a family with her.

"On Stone, I never meant to hurt Precious or you but at the same time, you even said it yo'self that she was treating you while you were locked up, fucking yo' homie, not bringing yo' daughter to see you. Plus, before you caught them cases, you was treating shorty like she wasn't shit. Now, she gone and you all of a sudden care. On BPSN, I'm starting to see that you one fake ass nigga," Nut snapped.

"You know what. cuuuz?" Mo Money said, stressing the cuz. "It is what it is. I told you I wasn't on that but since you forcing my hand, I'ma treat you like I never loved you," he threatened not scaring Nut in the least bit.

"Well, go put yo' kids up and come play ball," he shot back smirking,

"Bye King. Bye Paradise," he said waving as he walked off.

"Bye Nut! I love you!" Paradise yelled as Mo Money put her in the backseat of his car and strapped her in her car seat.

"Aw yeah, I saw yo' boy Bang with Reesie the other day. I tried to kill both of they hoe asses," Nutso told Mo Money as he climbed in the car.

"Don't make me kill you lil cuz," he replied ignoring his last statement. He pulled off before Nut could respond.

After dropping his kids off at home, Mo Money decided to stop over at Ashley's house.

"What's up, my little Ostrich?" He joked calling her by the pet name he made up for her when they were teenagers.

"Hey," she replied closing the front door and locking it.

"Have you been standing on that business for me?"

"Yeah," she replied with a hint of irritation in her tone.

"Damn, why you say. it like that?" Mo Money asked, frowning.

"Because you know that I don't want to be involved in anything like that."

"I told you a million times already that you gon' be good," he replied walking through her house, looking around as if he was searching for something.

"What are you looking for?" She asked from behind him. "Who been over here?"

"Nobody," she replied quickly, causing him to turn around to face her.

"If I ask you again and you lie to me, I'ma think you on some funny shit."

"Boy ain't nobody been over but a few of my friends."

"Which friends?"

"Does it matter? When did you start keeping track of who I let in MY house?"

"That lame ass nigga been over here?" Mo Money asked, looking at the ashtray that sat on the nightstand next to Ashley's bed. It had a few cigarette butts in it and she didn't smoke cigarettes. Her friends had no reason to be in her room smoking so that left one reason for the butts to be in the ashtray.

"Who?" Ashley asked, pretending like she didn't know who he was talking about.

"Dolla, bitch stop playing with me!" Mo Money growled angrily.

"He came over here to talk to me and apologize for what he did to me but I wasn't trying to hear that shit."

"Why was he in yo' house and in yo' bedroom if you wasn't trying to hear it?" He asked. He was so mad that he felt like he would literally explode at any moment.

"He forced his way in," she lied.

"So, why didn't you call me?"

"Because I didn't want you hurting him in my house."

"Where he living at?"

"I don't know," she replied quickly with a shrug. The problem was that she wasn't looking him in his eyes so he knew she was lying. Whenever she lied, she avoided eye contact.

Mo Money smacked his lips and shook his head in disgust. "This the same nigga that almost beat yo' goofy ass to death. He left yo' stupid ass in the hospital unconscious and now you protecting him?" He asked curling his lip up.

"I'm not protecting him," Ashley lied again. This time she felt bad about lying to him because he had a valid point.

"I was there for you every single day until you healed up. That nigga ain't even pay you a visit to apologize for what he did to you and you really right here protecting this nigga? I can't believe you," he said with a shocked expression. He was trying to play on her feelings so he could get Dolla's location. His words made sense and they made her feel bad in so many different ways.

"He stay in Calumet City," Ashley said almost in a whisper like it hurt for her to give up his location.

"Where?" Mo Money asked with a devilish grin on his face. This time, his fangs were showing vividly.

After getting Dolla's location, Mo Money met up with Breezy, Lil Dav and Lil Rodney and they made their way to Dolla's apartment building.

"So, we just bout to beat this nigga ass?" Lil Rodney asked, making sure they were all on the same page. He knew the three men he was with could be very unpredictable.

"Yeah," Mo Money replied with a nod.

"'Who is he?"

"Do it matter?"

"I'm tryna see why we fuckin him up," Lil Rodney asked and Mo Money pulled over.

"You want to get out of something?" He asked angrily.

"Naw"

"Aight then chill, Solid. You throwing me off," Mo Money replied. They drove the rest of the way in silence. When they made it to Dolla's building and to his apartment on the second floor, Mo Money lightly tapped on the front door.

"Who is it?" He heard Dolla yell from the inside of the apartment. He didn't respond. He just tapped on the door again. When Dolla swung the door open, Mo Money and his boys rushed him. They beat him brutally, hitting him with whatever they could get their hands on. The sight of Mo Money sitting on top of Dolla punching him viciously caused Lil Rodney to stop and watch. Mo Money had a crazed, deranged, spaced out look in his eyes. A look of pure hatred but the slight grin he had on his face said that he was enjoying every punch he threw.

"We gone!" Lil Rodney told him when he noticed that Dolla's face was so swollen and disfigured that you couldn't recognize him. He had to grab Mo Money off of him and hold him in a bear hug for him to stop.

"Hoe ass nigga!" Mo Money growled kicking him in his face before upping his Glock 31.

"Don't even do it moe," Lil Rodney told him. He thought that they were coming to deliver a simple message by kicking ass.

"Fuck this soft ass nigga," Mo Money replied before pumping five shots in Dolla's face. Breezy, Lil Dav and Lil Rodney jetted out of the apartment to the car but Mo Money stood there admiring his work. His beef with him went back years and it was personal. He felt good killing him. On his way out of the apartment, he saw a Chanel bag that he knew he had bought for Ashley, indicating that she'd been over there. He smiled because he knew that he had just ended that chapter of her life.

***

41

Hot Rod and Powder sat on the front porch of the trap on 105th. By now, none of Reesie's men worked in the spot. All of the workers were guys that Powder had brung into the fold.

"It be dry as hell right here," Powder complained flaming up a wood.

"That's because everybody be in the back of the building or on the side block right there," Hot Rod replied pointing to the corner of 105th Place. "This a lowkey block, plus this how I like it. I don't want them goofy ass niggas over here slowing up our money."

"I be tryna see some thots or something."

"You tryna slide to the building and see what's up?"

"Hell yeah," Powder replied with a smile.

Before making to the back of the building, Hot Rod and Powder seen that everybody was posted on 104th and Maryland. It looked like it was a block party going on out there. Hot Rod knew it was a lot of guns out there due to them being at war with more than a few different hoods and for that reason he didn't plan on hanging out there for too long.

"Aye, Hot Rod!" Reesie called from the porch he was sitting on surrounded by a group of men and women.

"What's up, Foe?" Hot Rod asked, approaching the porch followed by Powder.

"What y'all on?" Reesie asked after taking a sip from his double cup. He was always sipping lean. That was his drug of choice.

"Shit, we came over here to see what y'all was on."

"We ain't on shit. These niggas was just talking about playing cards. It's crazy, because on the Foe, I was just telling these niggas that they couldn't fuck with me on the Spades," Reesie said to Hot Rod before turning to Cello. "My partner here now, who tryna play for a thousand a game?"

"Let's do it," Cello replied raspily.

"Aight, send a mufucka to the G to get some cards," Reesie told him before turning back to Hot Rod. "You ready to check a few racks off these card dummies? I know you still got that janky ass shake on you."

"Come on man, you know that," Hot Rod replied with a smile. They used to Spades partners when they were cellies so they had chemistry.

"If we catch you tryna set the deck its gon' be a problem," Racks said to Hot Rod.

"Do you got enough money to play a G a game? "Hot Rod shot back

"Me and you can play for five thousand a game and see who bag the biggest."

"Bet," Hot Rod said with a grin.

An hour later, Hot Rod and Reesie were up four games and Racks was frustrated by how Cello was playing. He was making small mistakes that were costing them the book.

"Book they ass moe!" Reesie yelled slamming the King of hearts on the card table they had out there.

"Why the fuck you ain't hit the diamonds back?" Racks shrieked." On the Four Corner Hustler, yo' ass a fuckin bum!" He yelled throwing his remaining cards in Cello's face after they got booked for a yard that they had easily if he played the right suit.

"On the Foe, you tweaking now!" Cello snapped, standing up. "I clapped niggas for doing less than that," he said pointing at Racks.

"Man, shut the fuck up," Racks said, waving him off before turning to Hot Rod. "I quit and I'm not paying shit!" He said, making Hot Rod grimace.

"You got me fucked up. You better start workin some extra packs or go hit a stain or something because I need my bread before I pull out," he replied calmly. He wasn't going to get loud or none of that extra shit. A real gangsta didn't have to do any of that. If the time came when he had to show

how he was coming for his respect, then he would do what he had to do.

"I said what I said," Racks replied.

"You can put all that tough Tony shit in yo' back pocket and go get my mufuckin' money."

"I got you Moe man," Reesie said sensing that Racks was on bullshit.

"Hell naw, I don't want yo' money. I want his," Hot Rod replied jabbing a finger at Racks.

"You not getting shit from me unless you take it and a nigga ain't never took shit from me, on the Foe," Racks replied

"Here bro," Reesie said passing Hot Rod a wad of hundred-dollar bills.

Hot Rod looked at the wad of blue-faced hundreds like they were infected with an contagious disease and refused to take it.

"So, you not about to pay me my bread?" He asked. His nostrils were flared and his anger was starting to get the best of him. All eyes were on them. Everybody knew how Racks was coming but they were trying to see who this guy was who was matching his aggressive energy. They weren't used to seeing that.

"Get that shit in blood."

Hot Rod looked over and peeped that Powder had positioned himself behind Racks with his hand near his waist. He was waiting on him to give him the greenlight but Hot Rod knew if they killed Racks right then and there, then they would either get killed too or end up in jail. It was inevitable. Racks had made the list. He was going to get what he had coming for sure. He just had to figure out how he could do it without Reesie knowing about it. He shot Racks a look that could kill before grabbing the wad of money from Reesie and throwing it in the air, letting it blow in the wind.

***

44

Meanwhile, Mo Money, Von D and Lil Dav were in a stolen grey Acura looking for somebody to shoot.

"What the fuck?" Mo Money said as Von D turned up 104th and Maryland to see a whole bunch of hundred dollar bills floating in the air and on the ground. He was excited to see that it was a lot of people but they were distracted by whatever was going on. He armed his Tech out the passenger's side window. "What the fuck Bang doing over here?" he asked while applying pressure to his trigger. Seeing Bang only succeeded in infuriating him causing him to aim at aim trying to hit him and only him.

***

When the shots went off, Hot Rod quickly ducked behind the brick structure of the porch before upping his Glock and returning fire at the truck. Reesie, Racks, Lil 4 and Powder did the same thing. Once the Acura got towards the end of the block, it stopped and Mo Money along with some other guy hopped out still shooting at the crowd.

"Hot Rod!" Powder yelled, grabbing Hot Rod's attention. He looked over to see that Powder had an open shot on Racks.

"Don't do that!" Cello warned, peeping game as Mo Money and his homie jumped back in the Acura and screeched off.

***

Bang sat in the backseat of Lil Mike's car. They were in the middle of a drug transaction when his phone went off.

"What's the demo, Law?" He answered the FaceTime call from Mo Money.

"So, that's how you coming Law?" Mo Money asked with his face screwed up.

"What you talking about?"

"What the fuck you doing over there with Reesie nem?" Mo Money asked causing him to frown up at the camera.

"Goofy ass nigga, I'm in traffic with Lil Mike. What the fuck is you talking about?"

"Nigga, I just came from over there. What you think I'm blind or something?" Mo Money asked.

Bang simply handed his phone to Lil Mike.

"Yoooo," Lil Mike said looking into the camera.

"What's the demo, Law? Where y'all at?"

"We on 62nd."

"How long y'all been down there?"

"I been in the hood all day but I been with Bang for like a hour doe."

"Straight up?"

"On Stone."

"All well," Mo Money said before hanging up on Lil Mike.

Chapter 4
Mind Games

"Used to be my dawg you was in my left titty. Screaming ride or die thought that you a die with me," Mo Money rapped with DMX as he stood over the stove cooking a few ounces of coke. He was in his zone until he heard his front door open and close.

'Who the fuck was that?' he thought. He knew that Deja and the kids were at his mom's house.

"What's the demo, Law?" Bone asked entering the kitchen to see Mo Money pointing his Glock. His mouth hung open as he stared at Bone, who looked younger than he did last time he'd seen him.

"Cat got yo' tongue lil nigga?" A familiar voice asked as T Stone came into view.

"What the fuck?" Mo Money mumbled pointing his gun at T Stone who had a small smirk on his face.

"Damn, I really thought that you a be happy to see us," T Stone said stepping closer to him. Both him and Bone were dressed in expensive designer outfits like they had just came from a funeral.

"Y'all supposed to be dead," Mo Money said confused and scared.

"Finish singing that song," Bone said speaking in his usual, slow slur.

"What?"

"Finish singing the fuckin song," Bone urged raising his voice.

"Used to be my dawg you was in my left titty. Screaming ride or die thought that you a ride with me—"

"Found out you a bitch, you ain't even ride with me," T Stone rapped cutting Mo Money off.

"Now, it's a war you ain't on the side with me," a third voice said before Nut stepped in. He was accompanied by Killa.

"Killa?" Mo Money asked not believing his eyes. At this point, he was beyond scared. These were all men who he had history with. He had either killed them or stabbed them in the back.

"That's a decent ass song. I'm sure you can relate to the shit he was talking about," Nut said. He was the only one that was dressed in a Nike Tech with a pair of all white low top white Air Ones.

"I used to be yo' dawg, right?" Bone asked.

"I found out you was a bitch. You ain't ride with me against Lopez," T Stone spoke up.

"What the fuck y'all want from me?" Mo Money asked sounding like Steel off *'Juice'*.

"We came to take you home, Law," T Stone said.

"Shit, I am at home."

"Naw, Lil Dre, you got a nice ass home in Hell waiting on you. I think it's time for you to move in," Killa said.

"Come on," T Stone said taking another step towards Mo Money. He squeezed his trigger and put two hollows in T Stone's face.

"Damn bro, you shot me, again," T Stone said laughing. He didn't even flinch when the bullets hit him.

"There you go shooting people again," Killa told him making his way towards him. "Give me that gun," he said. Once he got within arm's reach, Mo Money put three shots in his chest.

"Damn, he tryna kill us again," Killa told the rest of the guys. That's when it hit Mo Money. He was the reason why Killa and T Stone were dead.

"Fuck," Mo Money gruffed and took off running. As he rounded the corner leading to his living room, he bumped into Sauce and D Thang.

"Where you going?" Sauce asked, grabbing him in a tight bear hug.

"Ain't no more running, Law," Bone said snatching the gun out of his hand and putting the barrel to his head. "Snake ass nigga," he said before popping the clip out of the gun. "D Thang gon' head and do you," he told Reesie's lil brother, who Mo Money had killed on accident.

D Thang pulled out a long machete. I want his trigger finger," he told the group of men who had forced Mo Money to a nearby table and laid his hands flat on the surface.

"Arghhhh!" Mo Money yelled in agony when D Thang chopped off all ten of his fingers.

"Oops," he chuckled as Bone stepped up.

"Help me cuz," Mo Money whimpered to Nutso who stood there watching with a small smile on his face.

"Shut the fuck up," Bone gruffed before saying, "I want his tongue for all the lies he told."

T Stone grabbed Mo Money's dreads and yanked his head back forcefully before forcing his mouth open. Mo Money tried to break free of their grasp but they were too strong. He watched in horror as Bone pulled out a scape. When he sliced his tongue out, he tried to scream but an inhumane gurgle came out instead.

"You know bro," T Stone said pulling out a Glock 20," That snake ass shit you did to me. I didn't even see it coming. You got me good," he told Mo Money before shooting him in his left eye.

"ARGHHHHH!!" Mo Money made a noise that was close to a scream as blood oozed from his mouth. T Stone then shot him in his other eye and he jerked and convulsed hoping that he just hurried up and died. For some reason, he felt full of life, even without eyes it was as if he could see the whole room smiling at his pain.

"How does it feel to get stabbed in the back?" Killa asked jabbing the machete in and out of his back. Blood was everywhere as he got mutilated by men who he'd wronged in the past.

"End this shit, cuz." T Stone told Nutso handing him a M-16.

"This the same gun I smoked Precious with," Nut said smiling as he checked out the rifle before putting the end of the barrel to Mo Money's chest right over his heart.

"Used to be my dawg you was in my left titty," they all said in unison before he pulled the trigger. Instead of dying, Mo Money woke up from his nightmare drenched in sweat.

"Damn," he mumbled wiping his sweat covered face with the palm of his hand. His eyes darted around the room looking for any sign of danger. Deja slept undisturbed beside him. That was a surprise because he never failed to wake her after having that same reoccurring nightmare. He had been having that same nightmare for the past two years. He climbed out of bed, grabbed his Glock and went to his kids room. He eased the door open and absorbed the peace that he got from being in their presence. Next, he did what he always did after having the nightmare. He checked his whole home with his Glock in his hand and his finger wrapped around the trigger. After making sure that his home was secure, he went back to bed and laid there staring at the ceiling until he dozed off.

***

Nutso, Binky, Arab and Flock sat in the front room of Arab's house, rotating two exotic stuffed Backwoods.

"So, you and Money into it for real or is y'all just mad at each other for the moment?" Arab asked Nutso the question had been on his mind, and he needed to know the answer. He just couldn't believe that Nut wanted Mo Money dead. It was hard to fathom.

"On BPSN, I'm not playing with him," Nutso replied with a frown. "That nigga tried to take me out this shit."

"So, it's no way that y'all would be able to fix that shit?"

"Yeah, he gotta let me unplug the machine that's keeping him alive," Nut joked making Binky and Flock erupt in laughter. "Naw for real doe would we be on good terms if the machine that he unplugged was really the one that was keeping me alive?" He asked.

"You got a point," Arab replied.

"What made you ask that?"

"Because I'm tryna figure this shit out," Arab paused to hit the wood a few times. "I knew you for a long time and I know the relationship y'all had so I'm tryna understand why you would tell me that it was him and Bang who smoked my pops?" He asked before taking another pull off the wood and handing it to Flock.

"Because if I knew and I didn't tell you that would make me just as bogus as they are, right? And not only that, I'ma be real, I been having a hard time catching his hoe ass and I know it wouldn't be that hard for you," Nut admitted.

"How do you know for sure that Mo Money and Bang did that shit?"

"It's obvious," Nutso said with a shrug. "That got their names written all over it."

"I'ma kill one of them niggas," Arab vowed.

"I saw Bang on Risky Road with the Foes not too long ago so he probably opp Mo Money before we get to do it."

"Fuck them niggas. What's up with this money?" Flock asked Nut.

"Whatever drugs y'all come up on, bring them to me and its gon' get sold. No ifs, ands, or buts about it."

"And what's the catch?" Arab asked.

"Ain't no catch. As long as y'all putting pressure on them hoe niggas with me, I'ma make sure any drugs y'all come across get sold. We partners. Y'all scratch my back and I'ma scratch y'all's. I don't need no money. I just want to smash Moe nem," Nut said passionately.

"Say less."

The next day, Arab and Flock were creeping through the 100's looking for Mo Money. Arab felt that since he supposedly set his father up, he was gonna be the first one that they smoked. He had a Millenium .45 on his lap anxious to avenge his father's death.

"Call him and see where he at. The nigga don't know what's going on. He gon' think shit all well," Flock suggested and Arab did just that.

"Hello?" Mo Money answered on the first ring.

"What's the demo, Law? Where you at?"

"I'm in the 100's. What you on?"

"I'm tryna link. Drop your Lo."

"I'm on something right now, Law."

"I got a nice lick lined up. I know you tryna get involved," Arab lied trying to play on Mo Money's greed.

"I got something nice lined up too. That's what I'm putting together right now."

"Damn, and you didn't invite me?" Arab asked feigning hurt.

"Naw, it ain't like that gang. It's Bang stain. He just need me to make it happen. You know I woulda called you ASAP if it was my lick," Mo Money lied quickly. Arab always put him on good stains so he didn't want to upset him and burn his bridges.

"You in the hood?" Arab asked riding past 105th and Cottage Grove.

"Yeah, I mean, naw," Mo Money replied quickly. "Let me hit you right back," he said before abruptly hanging up.

"That nigga a straight bitch!" Arab gruffed, turning up 105th and Eberhart knowing that Mo Money liked playing quiet blocks like that. Everything between Risky Road and D Block, between Cottage Grove and Prairie, from 103rd to 107th was basically free land. There weren't anybody claiming those blocks.

"Fuck it, since he wanna act like a hoe, I'ma smoke one of his homies," Arab told Flock looking at a crowd of men that were posted on 107th and Forest. "Aye, y'all know where I can find some Za at?" He asked the crowd, stopping in the middle of the street.

"We got some OG, thirty dollar trey-fives," A dark skinned guy with a nappy fro said.

"Let me get two for the fifty," Arab replied. He watched the guy run through a gangway and return. He approached the car without a worry in the world. When he got close enough, he leaned in the window to see the .45 that Arab was holding.

Arab smiled, "Where Mo Money at?" He asked.

"I - I don't know," the guy stammered and Arab applied pressure to his trigger, hitting the guy in his chin and neck before screeching off before anybody could return fire.

***

"Man, y'all smoked Sleepy lame ass. He not on shit. He not even one of the Moes," Nutso told Arab and Flock laughing at their failed hit. Binky was laughing so hard that tears were falling from his eyes. They were in one of Nutso's spots weighing up some heroin that Arab had come up on earlier that day.

"I don't care who he was. I was just sending a message," Arab replied with a shrug.

"That's not sending a message," Binky said. "Sleepy one of the Foes. Mo Money hate Foes and even if you did catch one of the niggas he got working for him. he wouldn't care.

He got them niggas out there to catch the bullets that's meant for him," he explained.

"So, what you saying I should get his OG?" Arab asked causing, Binky to smile but Nut frowned at his question.

"Keep my auntie out that shit," he replied sternly.

"They killed my pops," Arab shot back not breaking eye contact with him.

"Yo' pops was in the streets. My auntie ain't got shit to do with nothing."

"My brother ain't have shit to do with nothing either."

"And how you know?" Nutso asked. He felt like Arab was tweaking trying to justify going after his auntie and he was starting to take that shit personal.

"I know he ain't never did shit to Mo Money or Bang."

"And Bang lil sister ain't do nothing to nobody either. She was a little girl who got killed for nothing. What you saying?" Nutso asked screwing his face up.

The tension in the air was growing thick. The room grew awkwardly silent before he spoke again.

"Mo Money and Bang. Them the two mufuckas we at. We not gon' play they game and hit a bunch of innocents," he said pulling out a wad of money from the Dior bag he was carrying. "This for that D. Let me know when you come up on some more shit," he told Arab dropping the wad on his table before walking out.

After leaving out, Nutso went to go drop off Binky and pick up his girlfriend, Brittany. Since Lexi's death, Brittany was the only woman who he'd been dealing with. He had strong feelings for her that he tried to fight because honestly love was the last thing on his mind.

"What's up, lil lady?" he asked her as they entered Dave and Buster's. The game room was crowded with people from old to very young. "I hope you know I'm not finna take it easy on you," he joked with her as they started a game of Air Hockey.

Brittany stood around 5'9. She had long hair and rich chocolate colored skin. She wasn't the typical ratchet hood bitch. She was a registered Nurse who had a feisty side. She balanced Nut out in so many ways. He was grateful to have a woman like her in his life. He had his long dreads fishtailed so they wouldn't be in his face. He hit the puck hard knocking it off the table.

"Boy, you weak as hell," Brittany teased him while retrieving the puck and serving it.

"So, have you thought about what I asked you?"

"About me moving in with you?"

"Yeah."

"Yes but ..."

"But what?" Nutso asked, raising a brow.

"But I haven't made a decision yet. I want to but I know how you are and that's the only thing holding me back," Brittany replied.

"How am I?"

"You belong to the streets. You rip and run the streets all day and night so I feel like me moving in with you would be the same as me living by myself."

"Don't do that," he replied with a small smirk on his face.

"Don't do what? I'm only telling you what you already know."

"I'm tryna take this relationship to the next level. I already know you but I want to get to know you better—" Nutso was saying until somebody threw him in a tight chokehold from behind. He tried to wiggle his way out of the hold but his aggressor had a firm grip on him.

"What's up, pussy?" A familiar voice asked him from behind once he let him go.

"Stop playing with me you bitch ass nigga!" Nutso barked, turning around to see Mo Money smiling at him.

"Who is this pretty young lady?" He asked smiling at Brittany.

"Don't worry about who she is," Nutso said looking around the game room. He knew if Mo Money was there, something had to be up. He kicked himself for not having at least Binky or Mck Reese with him.

"Who you looking for?" Mo Money asked, leaning on the air hockey table. "I'm here with Paradise, King and Deja. Its King's birthday in case you forgot," he explained, relieving Nut of his worries.

"I'm glad I ran into you doe, lil cuz. I need a new Heroin connect. I know I'm good for it," he said flashing that wicked smile of his. Nut wanted to kill him right then and there but he remained calm.

"You not good for shit," he replied with a chuckle.

"Damn, cuz you still on that weird shit, huh?" Mo Money asked before turning to Brittany, "Yo' boyfriend the type that can hold grudges for years. Did you know that?" He asked.

She didn't respond. She just stared blankly at him trying to figure out what was going on. She didn't know who he was but she was going off her man's vibe and she didn't like this character.

"So, what's up Nutty? You gon' let bygones be bygones or is you still tryna play G.I Joe?"

"On Stone, you know what it is," Nutso replied flatly.

"You got this beautiful young lady right here. I'm sure she deserves all of you and we all know you can't give her that if you tryna play the field."

"Get the fuck on!" Nut spat. He was getting more and more angry with every second he spent in front of Mo Money.

"Okay," Mo Money replied throwing his hands in the air in mock surrender. "Did you tell her about Lexi?" He asked causing Nutso to stiffen up. You should hear what happened to Lexi it's a sad, sad story and its crazy cause she was a pretty girl just like you," he told Brittany, shaking his head slowly, like he was sad.

"Shut the fuck up!" Nut snapped raising his voice startling a few nearby kids."

Come on bae," he told Brittany, grabbing her hand and storming off. He made sure he bumped into Mo Money as he passed him.

"Don't make history repeat itself!" He yelled to Nut, watching him leave Dave and Buster's.

So, who is Lexi?" Brittany asked Nutso once they were inside his Hellcat Challenger.

"So, you really gon' feed into dude bullshit?" He asked shooting her a look of irritation.

"Who was he?"

"My big cousin. We used to be like brothers until he tried to kill me on some backdoor shit."

"Why would he do something like that?" She asked and he fell silent as images of Precious attacked his mind.

"Its a long story," he replied hoping she'd catch his vibe and leave it alone."

"Well luckily we've got nothing but time."

"Man, fuck that nigga!" Nut spat startling her. "My bad baby I just don't want to talk about that shit right now. It's a sensitive topic," he said before cutting up the volume to the Boothie Bucks song that was playing.

Chapter 5
Signs and Symbols

Mo Money, Bang, Lil Dav and one of Lil Dav's homies from the west side named, Fat Shorty sat in a stolen Jeep outside of a bank. All four men were dressed in all black from head to toe. Mo Money and Bang had their long dreads braided up and concealed under skull caps. Bang had a pair of dark shades on to hide his red eyes.

"Don't nobody need to get hurt in there. We going in with one job and that's getting the money and getting the fuck out," Mo Money told his team.

"You don't gotta keep saying that shit, bro," Bang replied.

"Shit, I know you not slow but I don't know about them," he replied nodding towards the backseat where Lil Dav and Fat Shorty sat. His phone going off stopped Lil Dav from responding.

Moments later, a masked up Mo Money rushed inside the bank with a Micro Draco in his hands.

"Tell them hoes to bag up all the money, no dye packs, no trackers, no marked bills! "He yelled aiming the Draco at the armed security guard's face. The element of surprise worked in his favor.

"Do it," The terrified, older black man yelled at the two tellers as Bang and the rest of the team ran in and locked the door behind them. When Lil Dav came in, he took the guard's gun and held him at gunpoint while Mo Money joined Bang and Fat Shorty behind the counter where the tellers were bagging up money.

"Where the rest of the money at?" Mo Money asked the taller teller, pointing the Draco at her pretty face. Both of the tellers were attractive women, who looked to be in their mid-twenties. The tall teller opened a door that led to the back of the bank. The backroom had a lot of lockers and safety deposit boxes along the walls. She gave him the key and watched in silence as he emptied out locker after locker. Bang had the other teller open a safe for him while Fat Shorty got all the cash out of the registers.

"Aye, should I grab all these quarters and shit too?" Fat Shorty asked after stumbling across rolls of coins.

"Hell naw!" Mo Money yelled back.

"I'ma just grab them for myself. Y'all better not ask for none either," he yelled back.

"Whatever dude," Mo Money mumbled getting annoyed. They were on a bank heist and this nigga was worried about some mufucking quarters.

"Don't hurt us," The taller teller told Mo Money calmly.

"Shut up," he replied before taking her back up front. "Is this everything?" He asked.

"Yes," both of the tellers replied in unison.

"Where the money the Brinks truck supposed to be picking up?" He asked and both women grew quiet.

"Where the fuck the money at?" Fat Shorty growled, grabbing the taller teller by her hair and smacking her with so much force that she almost fell.

"What the fuck is wrong with you?" Mo Money growled. He was so mad you could almost see the fire in his. eyes. "Look," he said turning to the shorter woman. "Tell me where that shit at or I'ma shoot yo' fucking face off," he promised. She must've seen the seriousness in his eyes.

"Come on," she told him, leading him back into the back room. She went to the rug, lifted it up to reveal a vault in the floor. "Are you going to kill us?" She asked and Mo Money could tell that this was the scariest moment of her life.

"Naw, y'all good, baby girl. I just want the money, I promise," he told her watching her open the vault. "If it's a gun in there, just leave it alone because I would hate to have to kill you for trying to save the day," he warned her.

She pulled out three duffle bags that were stuffed with money. Mo Money grabbed the bags. He handed two to Bang and threw one over his shoulder.

"We gone!" He told his team before dashing out of the bank. Before making it out of the bank, he locked eyes with one of the tellers and immediately felt bad for her. Lil Dav hit the guard with the butt of his Draco knocking him out cold. He grabbed the last two bags and rushed out of the bank. Before everybody could get into the Jeep, Mo Money shot Fat Shorty twice in his chest. He stumbled backwards and then fell to the ground in slow motion.

"What the fuck, bro!" Lil Dav growled, stepping towards Mo Money only to get stopped by Bang.

"His dumb, fat, stanking ass didn't listen. I said don't hurt nobody!" Mo Money yelled, pumping a shot in Fat Shorty's face before closing his door and jumping into the Jeep. "You coming or staying here with him?" He asked Lil Dav who was stuck watching his homie bleed out. The sound of Mo Money putting the Jeep in drive snapped him out of his trance and he jumped in the backseat before Mo Money hastily fled the scene.

***

Hot Rod sat on the front porch of the trap on 105th and Corliss. He watched his men serve fiends up and down the block while other customers who were buying weight pulled up and got served too. None of Reesie's men hustled in the trap or on the block. Everybody who worked, worked because they knew him or Powder.

"What's the demo, Law?" Hot Rod yelled to the driver of a grey Maserati that had just parked in front of the trap.

"What's that deal?" B Moe replied, climbing out of the car. Powder, who was in his passenger's seat, got out with him.

"I ain't on shit. I came to drop off some work and I decided to stick around once I seen that Powder wasn't here. What y'all on?"

"Shit, we just came from buying some new blicks," Powder said excitedly. "I just grabbed a big ass .50 Cal. That bitch so chunky!"

"What's up with you?" Hot Rod asked B Moe, noticing the look of frustration that was plastered on his face.

"Shit, man that nigga Prince tweaking," he replied. "What happened?"

"He sold me some work that was stepped on like a mufucka and I want my bread back."

"So, what he talking 'bout?"

"He talking bout as long as I sold that shit it shouldn't matter how good it was but bro that shit was so garbage that I had to damn near give it away just to get it off. I'ma clap his ass if he don't give me my mufucking bread back," B Moe said seriously, causing Hot Rod's smile to flip into a frown. He looked at Prince as something like a father, the father he never had.

"Y'all tripping. We family. Y'all not gon' do all that over a few dollars," he replied.

"You need to holla at dude ass then because he most definitely ain't actin like we family," B Moe replied with a frown.

"If you made yo' money back, then just chalk that shit up as a loss."

"Hell naw! I paid thirty-five hundred for that shit and only made forty thousand. I usually check about fifty-two grand," B Moe replied flaming up a Newport.

"You made yo' money back plus some, so if you ask me both of y'all ass tweaking."

"Here come this goofy ass nigga," Powder said, nodding towards Racks who was approaching the trap with a mug on his face.

"What's up?" Hot Rod asked him, returning his mug.

"Who the fuck is all these niggas y'all got out here serving?" Racks asked.

"They the guys, why? What's up?"

"Where the bros we sent over here?"

"I don't know. Call them and find out."

"Naw," Racks said shaking his head. "Ain't no getting money over here if we ain't involved. On the Foe, y'all gotta clear this shit up."

"Bro gon' head and get the fuck from over here before you get yourself hurt," Hot Rod replied with a chuckle. He was tired of him bumping his gums.

Instead of responding, Racks quickly upped his Glock but not as quickly as Powder did.

"Blow that bitch!" Racks told him while aiming his gun at Hot Rod.

"Nigga you went for yo' shit first so I see this ending two ways. Either you can blow and get smoked or you can walk away and get smoked later. Either way it go, you gotta see me for upping that blick," Hot Rod said as a Matte white BMW X6 stopped in the middle of the block.

"What's up, Solid?" Lil 4 asked jumping out the backseat on the BMW clutching his Fn.

"These niggas out here tweaking, on the Foe," Racks told him, still pointing his gun at Hot Rod.

"Hot Rod, what's the problem now, Law?" Reesie asked after climbing out of the driver's seat of the BMW. He was started to grow tired of Hot Rod and Racks fake ass beef. They didn't even know each other well enough to seriously be into it.

"Dude came over here asking questions about shit that don't concern him and then he upped on me," Hot Rod explained.

"What was he asking you?" Reesie asked. He was talking slow and his eyes were low and red. He was no doubt high off Percs and Lean. He had his long dreads hanging freely down his back.

"He asking about who working and who ain't working."

"Bro, these niggas that's out here working ain't even from the hood!" Racks exclaimed.

"Aye Foe Buddy, I'm paying you yo' money and ain't never came up short. We don't got y'all shit hot so what's the problem?" Hot Rod asked Reesie.

"The problem is y'all thinking y'all taking over this block," Cello chimed in.

"Hell naw homie, it ain't like that. We getting money and we paying y'all to be out here, so how we acting like we taking over?" B Moe asked.

"Man I'm paying for the trap. I got my own work and as long as my people ain't out here doing no goofy shit, it shouldn't be a problem with them working," Hot Rod said.

"So, what about our peoples?" Lil 4 asked.

"They had they chance and they was fucking up now that shit dead."

"Y'all ass tweakin," Reesie said slowly after listening to everyone plead their case. "Racks, let them do them. Hot Rod got it under control," he said making Racks smack his lips.

"On the Foe, you been capping lately," Racks told him. "How?"

"Who shit is this? Ours or theirs?"

"MINES NIGGA!" Reesie snapped, raising his voice. "This ain't THEY shit. This ain't OUR shit. This MY shit nigga," he said stepping closer to Racks. It was rare when you seen Reesie this mad and usually murder followed his anger.

"Just leave that shit alone, Solid," Cello said grabbing his shoulder only for him to snatch away.

"Hell naw Foe, this nigga been left the hood and he been back for a few years now but what did he really do? What the fuck did he do for this to be *'OUR'* shit?" Reesie asked Cello.

"I put in work nigga. That's what I did!" Racks yelled. "When was the last time you caught a body? Mo Money damn near checked you and you still ain't got yo' lick back."

"On the Foe, you lying. You saying that like I don't slide or something."

"You get money, bro. That's it," Racks replied waving him off.

"I'm the reason why YOU getting money, you lame ass nigga," Reesie shot back with a chuckle.

"I'm the reason why you still got these blocks. If I wasn't standing on them niggas necks, Moe nem woulda been took all this shit."

"You sound dumb as hell, goofy ass nigga," Reesie scoffed. "How about you go fuck with Moe nem and see how long you live?"

"You threatening my life?" Racks asked, screwing his face up.

"Take it how you want to take it," Reesie replied not backing down.

"Say less," Racks replied flashing a small smile before storming off.

"What?" Reesie asked Cello who was looking at him funny. "You got something you wanna say?"

"You tweaking foe," Cello replied.

"I ain't tweaking shit. You niggas clearly got shit fucked up," Reesie replied before turning to Hot Rod, who was silently watching the show. "Y'all good, Moe?" He asked him.

"Hell yeah, but dude got one more time to up a gun or come at me sideways and I'ma give him what he looking for."

"You a man before you anything, Law. I don't know what's up with dude weird ass," Reesie said causing Cello to shoot him another funny look that he didn't catch.

"Say less. We good doe, broski,"

"Aight," Reesie said dropping a gang sign with him before walking to his truck followed by Lil 4 and Cello.

Hot Rod was pleased with the spectacle that they had just put on. He had plans for Racks and this was perfect for what he had in mind. It was time for a little game of divide and conquer.

***

Deja entered her home tired from a long day of work to see Mo Money and Ashley sitting in the living room, on the couch, having what looked like a deep conversation. The sight was enough to piss her completely off.

"What's up, baby?" Mo Money asked her nonchalantly like he didn't have another bitch sitting on her couch, a bitch that he used to be crazy in love with at that.

"Ain't shit up. What the fuck you got going on?" Deja asked with a mug.

"Shit, talking business," he replied before turning his attention back to Ashley. If he did notice Deja's angst, he didn't acknowledge it.

"So, you think everything all well?" He asked Ashley.

"I don't know but I hope so because I'm scared. I think that the whole thing was a bad idea," she replied.

Deja was in the kitchen pretending like she was looking for something to eat but she was really eavesdropping on their conversation.

"You can't be on that scary shit when the people interrogate you because they gone be on top of everything

you say. They can read body language and shit. They gon'
ask you the same questions just in different ways tryna catch
you up so you gotta be on point," Mo Money told Ashley.

"They already asked me a million questions. I basically
told them everything that happened."

"Okay, stick to whatever story you told them and don't
say shit else. They might wanna search yo' house too so I'ma
hold yo' cut of the money."

"Okay," Ashley replied with a nod.

"I told you that shit was gone be a walk in the park, didn't I?"

"Yes, but you did kill somebody, and you told me you
wasn't gon' do that," she reminded him playfully punching
him in his leg.

"That's only because he put his hands on you," Mo
Money replied, flashing a smile. That killed Deja. She
couldn't help but to frown.

"Is that right?" Ashley asked returning his smile.

"You know the vibes. You my R.O.D. right?"

"I'm always gon' be your Ride or Die, Dre," Ashley
replied smiling hard.

Deja had heard enough. They were getting disrespectful
at this point.

"It's time for your company to RIDE her ass up out of
here," she said barging into the living room.

"Don't do that," Mo Money told her as Ashley got up
from the couch.

"No, she' s right Baby… Dre. I need to go handle some
business anyway so I'll talk to you later."

"All well," Mo Money said before walking her to the
front door.

"You be killing me with all that jealous shit. I come home
and lay up with yo' stanking ass every night so you can miss
me with all that insecure shit," he told Deja plopping down
on the couch and grabbing a Black and Mild out of the
ashtray.

"Boy, I'm not insecure about shit. I just don't appreciate you having another woman in our home while I'm not here. How disrespectful is that? I wonder how you would've reacted if you came home and I was in here with another man."

"I woulda smoked him and beat the fuck outta you," Mo Money replied with a chuckle but was serious as a heart attack.

"Right, so that mean I should be beating yo' ass right now," Deja said flinching at him making him laugh. "What the fuck is so funny?" She asked.

"You so fucking insecure. I love that shit doe, it's cute. I guess it show just how much you don't wanna lose me."

"No, I just don't want to spend the rest of my life in jail for killing your ugly ass," Deja replied, still not smiling.

Before Mo Money could respond, his phone started ringing. "What's the demo, Law?" He answered after looking at the screen and seeing that it was Arab calling him.

"Where you at Moe?" He asked. He was in traffic with Nutso and Binky trying to catch a body. His body in particular.

"I'm in traffic right now, Law. What's the demo?" Mo Money lied.

"Where you at?" I'm tryna link."

"Ain't shit happening right now. I'm on something but you can drop yo' Lo and I could pull up on you in about thirty minutes."

"He lying!" Deja yelled sitting beside Mo Money.

"Who is that yo' BM?" Arab asked

"Hell naw. Just send me yo' Location and I'ma head yo' way whenever I'm free," Mo Money told him before hanging up.

"I'm tired of that hoe ass nigga!" Nutso gruffed angrily. He was tired of playing Cat and Mouse games with his cousin. He wanted to catch him and kill him.

"On Stone, he been spinning me every time I call and try to get up with him. It's like ever since he found out who my pops was, he been actin weird."

"He knows what he did so now he moving with caution," Binky explained.

"I haven't gave him any signs that I even know what went down. That nigger just scary as hell."

"He might be scary but being scary got him moving smart. Its keeping him alive," Nutso said. "Since he don't know that you know about him setting up yo' pops, he gon play the innocent role with you and fuck with you just to make sure you don't find out. His snake ass might even throw Bang under the bus to keep his name clean."

"Well, you know that nigga better than anybody else so I gotta take yo' word for it," Arab told Nut after a moment of silence.

"He gon' call you back tonight and when he do, that's his ass," Nutso replied before flaming up a wood.

***

"Keep doing it like that," Deja moaned. She was on her knees and elbows with her ass tooted in the air while Mo Money licked around her asshole while fingering her pussy. After their fight about Ashley, she was in her feelings and he knew how much she loved getting her ass ate so he decided to do it to make her feel better.

"I'm about to cum," she moaned. He was using his tongue to trace circles around her asshole. Upon hearing that he switched his attention to her pussy and began sucking her clit. Within minutes, her legs were shaking uncontrollably and she was having an orgasm.

"You happy now?" Mo Money asked standing over her. She was stretched out on the bed panting, trying to catch her breath.

"Yup," she replied with a smirk.

"Give me a kiss then."

"Nope, you probably ate that other bitch ass before I got here," she joked, making him jump in the bed on top of her. "Give me some kisses!" He said, wrestling her trying to kiss her lips. The couple wrestled and played in the bed until Mo Money's phone went off.

"I'm outside," Bang told him after he answered.

"Bae, I'm 'bout to go get up with Arab. I'm not gon' be long doe and when I get back, maybe we can run this shit back. I think it took too long for me to make you cum," he told Deja who wasn't smiling anymore.

"Whatever," she replied with an attitude. She was pissed that their good time was being interrupted for him to run the streets. It was something that happened often and she should've been used to it by now but it still stung.

Mo Money really wanted to stay in but Arab had been trying to get up with him for the longest now and he didn't want to keep giving him the run around.

"I'll be back," he told Deja before grabbing his Glock, putting it on his waist and leaving out.

After he left, Deja took a hot shower and made herself a big bowl of her favorite ice cream, New York Strawberry Cheesecake. The kids were at their grandmother's house so she had the house all to herself. She laid in her bed flipping through channels until she spotted a familiar face on the 9 o' clock news.

"Bank robbed. One man killed," she read the news segment aloud. She smiled to herself as she watched the woman on TV, who worked at the bank tell her story.

"That dumb ass bitch!" She said giggling before stuffing a big scoop of ice cream in her mouth.

***

"So, when you plan on splitting that bread up?" Bang asked Mo Money who was sitting in his passenger's seat as he drove through the trenches, on their way to meet up with Arab.

"Maybe in another week or so.

"What's up with shorty?"

"She cool. I holla'd at her earlier."

"You ain't got shit else lined up?"

"Hell naw," Mo Money replied shaking his head. "How about you?"

"Yeah, but not nothing big."

"Cut me in Ku!" Mo Money replied with a chuckle. "Hold on, this Arab calling me now," he said when his phone started ringing. "What's the demo?" He asked Arab through the phone.

"Where you at, Law?"

"On Stone, I'm on my way to you right now."

"My bm got a few of her buddies over here. These hoes drinking and shit they talking like they tryna do dicks!"

"On Stone, I most definitely can help them with that. I should be pulling up in about five minutes, Law."

"All well, just let me know so I can be outside."

"All well," Mo Money said before hanging up.

Bang smacked his lips. "Let smoke dude hoe ass," he said before flaming up a wood that he had just rolled.

"Who? Arab?"

"Yeah, I didn't know Nell was his pops. If I did, I woulda been clapped his ass."

"For what?"

"Ain't no telling what he done told Nell about me and my family. My lil sister got killed. He probably had something to do with that shit."

"Do he even know that it was smoke with you and his pops?"

"I don't know." Bang shrugged. "But if I find out that he did and he was with that shit, I'ma smoke his ass," he vowed turning up 66th and Langley.

"Where the fuck this nigga at?" Mo Money asked looking for Arab as Bang cruised up the block. He had already called Arab and told him that they were pulling up so be on point.

When they got halfway up the block, a burgundy Jeep Cherokee that was parked, started up and pulled behind them. At the same time, a dark blue Chevy Malibu stopped in front of their car. Two men hopped out of the Malibu and began shooting at their car.

"What the fuck!" Mo Money hissed, ducking down in his seat.

Bang thought about returning fire through the windshield but he remembered that they were blocked in, so he went to plan B. He stomped on the gas and drove full speed towards the car in front of them. He rammed the car, causing both of the shooters to dive out of the way. That gave Mo Money enough time to jump out the car with his gun blazing. Bang was right behind him.

"We gone, Law!" Mo Money yelled before taking off sprinting towards 63rd Street. He looked back in time to see Bang drop one of the men who was standing in front of the Jeep shooting at them. Bang took off after him. They both were familiar with the area so it didn't take long for them to make it to 63rd and Evans.

"Let's go to Timo crib," Bang suggested as they marched up. Evans constantly looking around for any signs of danger. When they made it to Timo's crib on 61st and Cottage Grove, he was standing in the front surrounded by No Law members.

"What's the demo?" Timo's older brother CB greeted Mo Money and Bang, shaking up with both of them. The No Laws were a group of Black P Stones who just like their name implied followed no laws. They did what they wanted to do.

"Y'all well?" Timo asked clutching his Glock. He sensed that something was up due to how hard they were sweating.

That plus the look on their faces let him know that some was going on.

"Somebody just tried to box us in on Langley and fuck us up," Bang told him.

"Damn, what folks nem was on?"

"I don't even think it was them to be honest," Mo Money said pulling out his phone and calling Arab. "Bro, what type of weird shit was that?" He asked once he answered.

"What you mean?"

"Mufuckas just tried to box us in over there. I know you heard the shots. That wasn't no random shooting. Somebody was waiting on me to pull up."

"So, what you tryna say I set you up?"

"I'm saying that somebody was waiting on me. Who all in that crib?"

"Just me, my BM and a few of her friends."

"And who did you tell that I was coming over?"

"I never said you in particular. I just said that I had a few homies on their way over."

"Why wasn't you on the porch waiting for me to pull up?"

"Fuck you mean?"

"You told me to call you before I pulled up so you could be on point and I called you way before I pulled up so you shoulda been out there waiting for me?"

"So what you saying, Moe?" Arab asked tired of Mo Money beating around the bush.

"I ain't saying shit bro," Mo Money replied with a chuckle. "It's all well, I'ma figure that shit out."

"Where you at right now?" Arab asked but instead of responding, Mo Money hung up in his face.

"So, what's up?" Bang asked Mo Money with a small frown on his face.

"I don't knows but I'm most definitely gon' find out," he vowed before calling a Uber to pick him up. Something wasn't right and he was going to keep his eyes open until he found out exactly what it was.

Chapter 6
The Cross

JB was a 28-year-old hustler that Powder had left in charge of overseeing the trap whenever he wasn't there. He was Powder's older cousin and was a great hustler but due to him always being in and out of jail, he never reached his full potential as a hustler.

JB was in the back room of the trap getting his dick sucked by a bop that he'd met earlier that day, when he heard the front door open and close. He didn't stop what he was doing because it was 2 AM and he knew that only Powder and Hot Rod had keys to the trap.

"I'm ready to fuck," he told the thick, brown skinned woman who immediately stripped naked and laid in the bed.

"What?" She asked JB after he stood there grinning at her for a moment.

"You not my bitch. I'm not getting on top of you and making love. Turn over and put that ass in the air," he replied and she did as told. He wasted no time sliding on a condom before sliding inside her from behind. The woman moaned softly while he hit her at a steady pace.

"You got some good ass pussy," he grunted, smacking her ass and picking up the pace of his strokes.

The woman started to curse and shout in pleasure while throwing her ass back matching his energy. She was so loud that he didn't hear the bedroom door open.

"You like this dick?" He asked, smacking her ass again.

"Yeeessss," she purred.

JB was about to say something else but the feel of cold steel on the back of his neck made him stiffen up. The woman he was fucking didn't notice that he had stopped stroking so she continued to work her hips.

"Where that shit at nigga?" A man's voice asked JB from behind. Upon hearing the voice, the woman turned around to see three masked men holding guns and she immediately started shrieking.

"Shut the fuck up, bitch!" The man who was wearing an Iron Man mask gruffed before shooting her in the head.

"We empty the trap every night. The only thing in here is probably a couple thousand dollars and maybe a half a brick," JB confessed.

"Get dressed," the guy wearing an Incredible Hulk mask said.

JB got dressed and led the men to the basement of the house. As he walked through the house, he noticed that two of his guys were tied up.

"This all we got in here," he said after cleaning out the stash. The third guy, who was wearing a Spider Man mask shot him in his stomach.

"Who the fuck you think you playing with nigga? Where the rest of that shit at?" Spider Man gruffed.

"On the G, that's it!" JB said holding his stomach.

"Go smoke everybody in this bitch," Iron Man told the other two guys. "So, you really want to die over some shit that ain't yours?" He asked JB once they were alone.

"One the G. On my son. That's everything that's in here. When that run out, I supposed to call Powder and he'll drop off more," JB replied while listening to gunshots that he knew were killing his friends.

"Facetime, Powder," Iron Man demanded, and he did as told.

"Aye Powder, some niggas ran in the spot—" was all JB got out before Iron Man shot him in his face three times.

Iron man picked up the phone and stared into the camera for a few seconds.

"Bitch ass niggas," he murmured before grabbing the pillowcase that he had stuffed with work and rushing out of the house.

When Hot Rod, Powder and B Moe arrived at the trap, they walked in to see something that they weren't prepared for. It looked like a scene straight out of an action movie. Niggas were stretched out, laying in puddles of their own blood.

"Damn," Powder said sadly, shaking his head.

"Hot Rod called Reesie and told him to pull up ASAP. He wanted him to see what he was seeing.

"Damn, bro. They even smoked some bitch. She naked. It look like she was getting fucked," Powder shouted from the backroom.

"Who you think did this shit?" B Moe asked Hot Rod.

"I don't know," he replied with a shrug. "But I do know that whoever did it, they didn't break in so they either knew how to get in without forced entry or it was somebody that the guys knew well enough to let in," he explained as Reesie entered the trap accompanied by Lil 4 and Cello.

"What the fuck happened?" Reesie asked looking around at all the dead bodies. He was high off Percs and Lean but the sight blew his high immediately.

"That's what we tryna figure out. Clearly somebody ran in this bitch and smoked all our guys. I would say that this was a robbery gone wrong but bro nem tied up so what could've possibly went wrong? This look like some personal shit," Hot Rod explained. "Don't none of it add up, doe."

"What make you think that it was something personal?" Cello inquired, raising a eyebrow.

"Because for one, I don't have any opps or niggas that want me dead and if it was y'all opps that ran in here, they would've noticed that nobody in here was from around here, you feel me?"

"That makes sense," he agreed reluctantly. He didn't care for Hot Rod due to his beef with Racks. He was siding with his day one over any random ass nigga. He didn't care how much Reesie fucked with him.

"I'm surprised that wasn't none of y'all guys outside to see something," Hot Rod said throwing some bait out there.

"It's dead as hell outside," Lil 4 spoke up with a slight mug on his face. He, just like Cello, didn't too much care for Hot Rod but he never aired his feelings out of respect for Reesie.

"I ain't gon' lie," Powder said running a hand over his face. "I feel like this was some backdoor shit," he said looking at Reesie.

"What you mean?" Reesie asked before hitting his double cup.

"I think it was somebody from around here that ran in our shit. It's clear that niggas don't fuck with us and don't want us over here getting money, especially that goofy ass nigga Racks. Y'all can sit right here and act like y'all don't know what the fuck going on but I know what I know!" Powder snapped.

"Shorty tweaking. We making our own money. A LOT of money, at that and we making money off y'all so what the fuck we need to rob y'all for?" Cello snapped back matching Powder's energy." That's some hoe ass shit. If we didn't want y'all over here we would've moved y'all lame ass around, on the Foe."

"I ain't never got moved around and I'll be damned if I let one of you soft ass niggas move me."

"So, what you saying?" Lil 4 asked, clutching.

"What you doing all that clutching for?" B Moe asked him, speaking up for his cousin.

"On the Four Corner Hustler, y'all see what happened to y'all people. Y'all better be cool," Cello gruffed, raspily causing both Reesie and Hot Rod to shoot him funny looks.

"What's that supposed to mean?" Hot Rod asked quickly pulling out his Glock 27. "You said that like you know something we don't know."

"Calm down, Law," Reesie told Hot Rod calmly, all while making a mental note to holla at him about all the pistol upping he was doing.

"Ain't no calm down," Hot Rod snapped. "This goofy ass nigga talking like he had something to do with my peoples getting smoked. You ain't gon' understand because you didn't know bro nem but we did," he said and Reesie knew he had a valid point.

"He been with me all night, so I know for a fact that he didn't come in here," he replied.

"But he knows who did it, don't you?" Hot Rod asked Cello, wrapping his finger around the trigger of his Glock.

"I don't know shit," Cello spat.

"I don't believe that," Powder chimed in.

"I don't either but what's done in the darkness always comes to the light and when it does," Hot Rod waved his gun at Cello, "Ima fuck one of you niggas up," he promised.

"Did y'all lose anything besides yo' peoples?" Reesie asked doing his best to hide his anger.

"Only half a brick."

"I'ma pay you for that."

"That lil shit ain't nothing," Hot Rod said, waving Reesie off. "If you wanna pay me, pay me in answers. I wanna know who did this."

"I'ma look into it for you but on the Foe, we ain't have shit to do with it," Reesie answered honestly.

"Where Racks at?" Powder asked.

"Shit, I don't know I haven't seen Foe since we had words. Why? You think he did this?"

"Hell yeah," Powder replied with a straight face.

"My brother a killer not a thief," Lil 4 chimed in.

"This damn sure look more like a murder scene than a burglary," B Moe retorted.

77

"Let these niggas think whatever they want to think. We know what it is. We gone," Cello said to Reesie.

"Hot Rod, I'ma put my ear to the streets and when I find out who did this shit, I'ma kill em' personally," Reesie promised before leading Lil 4 and Cello out of the trap.

Reesie and his men went around the corner to the building to Bands' apartment.

"Them hoe ass niggas capping, ain't they?" Cello asked Reesie, who was sitting on the living room's couch pouring himself another cup of Lean.

"All you niggas capping," Reesie gruffed. He was bothered by the situation because if Hot Rod would've reacted off his assumptions, they could've killed them before they even knew what was going on. Luckily, Hot Rod's love and respect for him was the utmost or else that whole situation could've played out differently. If one of his men had anything to do with that shit, they were going to feel his wrath because they put him in danger by not alerting him.

"On the Foe, I see I'ma have to clap one of them niggas," Cello replied while rolling up a wood.

"Fall yo' ass back bro."

"Fuck you mean fall back? That nigga just upped a gun on me. You got me fucked up."

"Think about what you said to him."

"It shouldn't matter what the fuck I said. This not they shit, this our shit," Cello replied, causing Reesie to chuckle.

"Where the fuck you niggas keep getting this 'OUR' shit from?" he asked.

"Nigga, I been through this bitch just as long as you have. I caught bodies for the hood and I did time for the hood. You better know that this OUR shit. You can try that chief shit with somebody else," Cello replied before flaming up his wood and taking a deep drag.

"Nigga, you ain't did half the shit I did," Reesie said waving him off. "You really riding my wave if we keeping it a buck."

Cello smacked his lips. "Foe, is you serious?" He asked shooting Reesie a funny look.

"On the Four Corner Hustler. I'm dead ass serious. I was shooting before every one of you niggas and I'm the one that put y'all in position to even think that you somebody. When you mention Risky Road, I'm the first name that comes to mind. This my shit."

"Yeah, that Lean fucking with yo' head," Cello scoffed.

"On the Foe, you niggas gone make me cut y'all water off," Reesie told him.

He screwed his face up but didn't respond so Reesie kept speaking. "Lil 4, did you call around and see if they saw anybody go in that crib?" He asked Lil 4.

"Yeah, everybody been saying that they haven't seen or heard shit," he replied.

"Why you so concerned with that shit, Foe?" Cello asked, he was irritated by how Reesie was acting.

"Because whoever did that shit didn't just take from Hot Rod, they took from me too and don't nobody take shit from Foe Buddy," Reesie replied speaking in third person.

"What if it was one of the guys?"

"I'ma cut they fuckin hands off."

"Yeah?"

"Yeah," Reesie confirmed firmly before turning to Lil 4, "I'm 'bout to buss a few moves. I'll be back in a minute. Call that nigga Racks and tell him to hit my line. He ain't been answering my calls or responding to my text," he said before leaving the apartment.

Cello sat at the dining room's table, smoking his wood in silence. He wasn't feeling how Reesie had been acting as of lately. All that chief shit and the way he was showing Hot Rod more love than he showed his day ones had him pressed. He planned on addressing the issue real soon.

Chapter 7
Blurred Lines

Deja laid in bed next to Mo Money. They had just finished a two hour long sex session and he was ready to go to sleep.

"You know I love you, right big head?" She asked him.

"Yeah, and I love you, too, long neck."

"Stop playing!" She said punching his arm. "Are you ready to extend our little family?"

"Why, you pregnant?"

"Not that I know of. I was only asking to see how you felt."

"I wouldn't mind."

"Would you mind leaving the city? It's too hot out here and I think we should go somewhere else and start fresh."

"You know what you know," Mo Money mumbled tuned into the basketball game that was on the TV.

"You know we gotta go to the party that my granny having for my brother tomorrow," Deja reminded him.

"Damn, that is tomorrow. What time doe?"

"I think it's at seven or eight."

"Bet, we gon' do it big for broski. On Stone."

"Don't do too much. My family already think you crazy," Deja said with a giggle just as his phone started vibrating. It was Ashley Facetiming him.

"Hey ugly," she said smiling into the camera after he answered.

"What's the demo?" Mo Money asked casually unaware of the daggers that Deja was shooting him. She didn't like the fact that he put their conversation on pause to Facetime another bitch.

"What you doing?" Ashley asked,

"Shit, laid up with bae right now. Its family time," Mo Money replied causing her to frown and Deja to grin. She liked what he had said to her so she decided to suck his dick while they were on Facetime.

"We need to talk."

"Speak, I can hear you. Deja busy so she not paying us no attention," Mo Money replied loving the deep throat that Deja was giving him. He was trying his best to keep a straight face.

"The police came and searched my house today."

"You ain't got shit there. You cool. Everything should be all well."

"They wasn't searching for money or nothing like that. They came about Dolla."

"So, what the fuck you telling me for?" Mo Money snapped flashing a mug.

"They were asking if I knew anyone who would've wanted to hurt him and when was the last time I seen him and spoke to him."

"On Stone, you called me to tell me that they questioned you about dude? Fuck dude!" Mo Money said harshly.

"It's more but we need to speak in person."

"I'm busy right now."

"Well, whenever you're done you need to get over here ASAP," Ashley said before hanging up on him.

"You not leaving back out tonight so don't even think about it," Deja told Mo Money, holding his dick in her hand, slowly stroking it.

"Yes I am."

"Well, I'm going with you."

"Okay, just finish what you started," he said grabbing a handful of her long hair. He didn't care about taking her with him because he knew he wasn't staying long. The only reason he was going was to see what Ashley had to say about the police investigating Dolla's murder. He didn't need to get wrapped up in that shit so he had to play it safe.

When Mo Money and Deja pulled up to Ashley's house forty-five minutes later, they saw her waiting on the porch wearing a silk Chanel robe that showed off her long, sexy legs. She headed towards his Infiniti truck not knowing that Deja was in his passenger's seat.

"Didn't I say that *'WE'* need to talk?" She asked frowning at Mo Money

"Yeah, what's the demo?"

"If I wanted to talk in front of her, I would've said whatever I had to say while we were on Facetime."

"Gone head and speak your mind. He gone tell me anyway," Deja told her.

"Dre, can we speak in private?" Ashley asked softly.

Mo Money looked over at Deja, who was giving him a look that said *'No'*.

"I'ma be right back," he told her, quickly opening his door and jumping out the truck. Ashley had a triumphant smirk on her face as she led Mo Money to her front door.

"Don't take your ass in that house!" Deja yelled out of her window, watching him walk up her steps.

"What's up?" Mo Money asked Ashley, looking down at her legs.

"Why did you bring that bitch to my house?" She asked with a frown.

"I told you that it was family time. I promised her that tonight was all about her."

"You always talking that R.O.D shit to me but you starting to show me that that's all it is, talk."

"Ashley, what the fuck is you talking about?"

"You be so quick to down me for fuckin with another nigga but you been playing house with that bitch for how long now?" She asked, putting her hands on her hips.

"First off, Ms. Loyalty Is Everything you—"

"I'm what?" Ashley asked, cutting him off.

Mo Money took a deep breath. "I didn't come over here for all that. I came to talk about the shit you was telling me about on the phone," he said not wanting to argue with her about their love lives. Right now wasn't the time for that.

"The police told me that they had some strong leads on who murdered Dolla."

"Did they mention me?" He asked, his heart rate had increased drastically.

"No."

"So, why you telling me?"

"Because I know that it was you who did it and I just wanted to tell you to be careful," Ashley replied causing him to smack his lips.

"What the fuck you mean *'you know I did it'*? I ain't do shit to that bitch ass nigga, you tweaking!" He snapped.

"Really Dre?"

"Yes, really. You called me over here to accuse me of killing that hoe ass nigga? You ain't right, Ashley. I'm gone," he said loudly before storming off.

"DRE!" Ashley called after him, but he waved her off and hopped in his truck.

"Fuck that bitch, baby," Deja told him as he pulled off leaving Ashley standing on her front porch confused and hurt.

The next day, Mo Money was out in traffic with Bang and Breezy. They were hitting blocks trying to find some trouble to get into. "We haven't slid on Reesie nem in a while. Them niggas got you ducking yo' shit?" Bang asked Mo Money, trying to gas him up.

"Stop it, bro," Mo Money replied flatly not even bothering to look up from his phone. "You know I stay going through that bitch acting crazy."

"Let's slide through that bitch then."

"On Stone, Von D just texted me and said Reesie driving up 105th right now heading our way," Mo Money told Bang and Breezy.

"There goes his truck right there," Bang said looking through the rearview mirror. Reesie pulled up on the passenger's side of Mo Money's car which Bang was driving. Mo Money was shocked at what he was seeing.

"Aye Bang," he said turning left to see Bang's gun pointed at his face. His heart dropped thinking that it was over.

"MOVE BRO," Bang gruffed, ready to pull the trigger. Mo Money leaned back and that's when Bang saw what he was seeing. His twin, Hot Rod was driving Reesie's Benz and Reesie was in the passenger's seat. The light turned green and Hot Rod pulled off without ever looking over. If he did, he would've seen that he was seconds away from catching a few bullets.

"On Stone, what type of games yo' brother playing?" Mo Money asked Bang with his face screwed up. "Better yet, when the fuck did that nigga get out?" he asked.

"He been out for a lil minute now but I didn't know that he was fuckin with Reesie nem."

"How come you never told me he was out?"

"I don't know," Bang replied with a shrug. "I haven't been rotating with him like that. He been on his own shit. Plus, I know that y'all don't fuck with each other so I didn't think it mattered to you."

"Facetime him."

Bang pulled out his phone and Facetimed his twin.

"Bro, what type of time you on?" He snapped when Hot Rod picked up. He was mad because he was two seconds away from accidently killing him.

"Fuck is you talking about, bro?"

"I was just about to dunk Reesie ass but it's you driving his Benz. What the fuck is you doing? When you start fucking with that nigga?"

"We were cellies when we was in the county, and why was you about to fuck him up?"

"I'm locked in with Mo Money. That's my brother so all his opps are my opps,"

"That's yo' brother?" Hot Rod asked with a chuckle. "That's the same brother that got our sister killed," he said pissing Bang off. He had a deep hatred for Mo Money and Nutso because he felt like they were the reason why their little sister had gotten murdered. That was another reason why he formed a bond with Reesie. They had a mutual opp.

"It's a lotta niggas that want Reesie and you riding around with him with the windows down like that bitch bulletproof. You tweaking," Bang retorted making Hot Rod smack his lips.

"Mannnn, Mo Money nem some straight hoes!" He shot back. Mo Money heard his comment and frowned up.

"On Stone, you tweaking bro," Bang said angrily.

"Look, lil bro I'ma be a hundred with you. Fuck Mo Money. That nigga got Mekiyah killed so if I catch him or anybody that's rocking with him, that's they ass."

"I'm rocking with him, on Stone," Bang said firmly.

"Well, don't get done how I did Blow," Hot Rod replied before hanging up on him.

Neither Bang nor Mo Money spoke a word for a while. They were both deep in thought. Bang was thinking about the last comment that his brother made. He had basically just admitted to being the one who murdered his best friend, Blow. If that was true, then Hot Rod had to pay.

"So, how this shit 'bout to go?" Mo Money asked Bang finally breaking the silence.

"I don't know but I'm not gon' front like I'd be okay with you or anybody else getting down on my brother. I know he be tweaking but he all I got besides my son."

"I feel you, gang and on Black Stone, I don't really got shit against yo' brother but I only got one life. I'm not gon play with it. If I get smoked who gon' take care of my family?" Mo Money paused and continued, "I'm not gon' sit back and let nobody take me out this shit. I don't care who it is."

"Ain't no question, bro. We gon' figure this shit out," Bang replied. His mind was all over the place.

Mo Money sat next to him, thinking about how he was going to kill Hot Rod as soon as the opportunity presented itself. He wasn't trying to hear nothing that Bang was talking about. Once you crossed that line, you had to stay there and Hot Rod was on the other side.

"Out of the love and respect I got for you, I'ma stay out yo' brother way," he told Bang, lying with a straight face.

"All well, but if he come yo' way I can't ask you not to protect yo'self."

"Fasho," Mo Money said. It got awkwardly silent for a while, while Bang drove aimlessly through the city.

"You well?" He asked him

"Hell yeah, that goofy ass nigga got my mufucking head hurting," Bang replied with a chuckle. He then drove to where his car was parked.

"In the AM, Law," he told Mo Money climbing out of his car.

"Aight, love, bro," Mo Money said getting out the passenger's seat and into the driver's seat.

Bang stopped and locked eyes with him. "Love," he said before climbing into his car.

Mo Money knew that he had to watch Bang close. Real close. Hot Rod was his blood and blood was thicker than water so he knew that. If it came down to it, Bang would choose his brother over him in a second. He would hate to have to smoke Bang but at the end of the day it was what it was.

After dropping Breezy off to Rodney and Lil Dav, Mo Money decided to stop by his mother's home in Chicago Heights.

"Who shit is this?" Mo Money asked himself looking at the silver Benz that was parked in his mother's driveway next to her car. He entered her home and went straight to the living room to see her sitting on the couch with a light skinned chubby nigga who he was familiar with. "Who the fuck is buddy?" He asked his mother while mean mugging the guy.

"You better watch your mouth in my house, black ass little boy," his mother shot back before saying, "Dre, this is my boyfriend, Tido, Tido, this is my disrespectful ass son, Dre."

"What's the demo?" Tido asked shooting Mo Money the same look he was shooting him.

"What's the demo?" Mo Money replied in a mocking manner. "The demo is you gotta roll up outta here."

"Boy, shut up!" Ms. Williams shouted embarrassed by her son's behavior. "Baby, give us a minute alone so we can speak," Tido told her politely. She didn't argue. She simply got up and shot Mo Money a mug before leaving the room.

"Look lil bro I don't know how you think this shit gon' play out but it's not gon' end how you think it is. All that aggressive, tough shit you on, you can put that shit in yo' back pocket and speak to me like a man or we don't have to speak at all," Tido told Mo Money in a manner that wasn't aggressive or passive.

"It really ain't shit for us to speak about. My OG don't need a nigga. I take care of her," he replied stubbornly.

"And I salute you for that, lil bro but you can't take care of her how I could. You can't give her the love and affection that she needs from a man. You not always available to listen to her vent or to clean up the house after she worked all day. You got yo' own life and she has hers. You're her son, not her father or her man."

"Look homie," Mo Money said running a hand over his face and taking a deep breath. "I understand what you saying but I'm not trying to hear that shit," he said shaking his head.

"You gotta understand that your mother is grown and you can't dictate her happiness," Tido said with a frown. "You come in here talking crazy. That's some kid shit. You call yourself a man. You gotta carry yo'self accordingly. If I didn't care for your mother like I do, then I would've reacted and matched your energy. I promise you, you wouldn't like that," he said causing Mo Money to frown up. "Yeah, I know all about you. You from them buildings on 104th Street behind Corliss High School. You had a good but short run selling drugs and now you robbing the city. You like playing with guns but you are not the only nigga out here that's built like that. It's a lotta steppers in the city," Tido added.

Even doe Mo Money felt slightly offended, he admired Tido's way of handling him. Tido had charisma.

"Where yo' from?" He asked.

"Moe Town."

"You one of the men?"

"Can't you tell?" Tido asked raising an eyebrow.

Mo Money cracked a smile and extended his hand. They shook up Black P Stone.

"Ain't you a lil too young for my OG?" He asked. Tido looked to be in his mid thirties and his mother was in her early forties.

"There you go worrying about the wrong shit again," Tido shot back. "But on some man to man shit, I think you should go apologize to her for how you came in."

"You don't know me like that to be making those type of suggestions," Mo Money replied seriously.

"There you go showing that child-like mentality again. A man shows the upmost respect at all times. You won't make it nowhere without respect, manners and a little class. Damn bro, I heard good things about you but you showing me otherwise."

Mo Money studied Tido with a small smirk on his face before saying," You right," And leaving the room to go talk to his mom.

"What, ugly?" Ms. Williams asked Mo Money when he entered her bedroom.

"Ma, you know how overprotective I am. I get jealous when I see you with another man. I apologize for how I acted. I love you, girl."

"I love you too, son." She flashed a warm smile that resembled his own.

"So, do he treat you well?"

"Yes, he does."

"Do you love him?" Mo Money asked unsure if he really wanted to know the answer.

"I won't say that much but he does make me happy. If dating him is a mistake, let me make that mistake and learn from it. Don't just try to snatch my happiness away from me. That's not fair to me. I do have a life."

"My bad, ma," he replied sincerely.

"Is everything okay with you? You looking rough. I might have to pat you down before I let you walk out," she cracked with a giggle.

Mo Money unconsciously ran a hand over his nappy dreads." Yeah, I'm all well, ma. I just wanted to come over and see that pretty smile of yours. You know that smile can turn my worst day around."

"Boy please, save that game for one of those thots you be chasing," Ms. Williams said laughing. Mo Money also laughed.

He always found it funny when she spoke like she was his age.

"How are my grandkids doing?" She asked.

"They good. They with Deja."

"Have you spoken to Nut lately?"

"Naw but I gotta go ma. I just wanted to come check on you," Mo Money said preparing to leave.

"Okay, son. Next time, call before you come. I love you."

"I love you too ugly," he joked giving her a hug and a kiss on her forehead. Before he left, he approached Tido who was in the living room watching Sportscenter. "Take care of her bro," he told him.

Tido stared at him with a blank expression for a few seconds before saying, "You don't need to coach me on how to be a man. You should focus on taking care of yourself because you looking a lil off," Tido replied with a small smirk on his face.

"Anybody ever told you that you got a smart ass mouth?"

"Smart or do I just say what's real?" Tido asked raising an eyebrow.

"I'm gone, man," Mo Money said with a chuckle, shaking his head as he left out the house. Tido was an interesting character and he was most definitely going to do his homework on him.

Chapter 8
Up the Score

Nutso laid in his king-sized bed next to Brittany cuddled up watching a movie on Netflix.

"I got something nice for you," he told her, jumping out of the bed. He went to his dresser, into his underwear drawer and rambled through it before coming out holding a jewelry box.

"What's this?" Brittany asked after he handed it to her. "Open it and see."

She opened the box and her hand shot to her mouth when she saw the expensive looking diamond choker.

"Thank you, it's beautiful," she told Nutso before leaning over and giving him a kiss.

"You like it?" He asked with a smile.

"Of course. How could I not?" She asked, still admiring the necklace.

"I didn't want to give it to you without nothing to go with it so I got you this too," he said, reaching under his pillow and pulling out another jewelry box. He opened it to show her a small rose gold Presidential Rolex.

"Oh, my God. Thank you so much," Brittany told him almost in tears. Nobody had ever bought her anything that nice.

"It ain't shit. You my baby. I'ma have you fuckin all them hoes up," Nutso replied with a smirk. "So, have you been thinking about moving in with me?"

"Yes, and I still haven't been able to convince myself that you love me enough to focus on our relationship more than whatever you're focusing on in the streets. I don't believe you're ready and I might as well stay in my own shit alone if I'm going to move in here and be alone."

"I told you a hundred times that it ain't gon' be like that."

"So, you're telling me that you're willing to fall back from the streets for me?"

"Yes," Nutso lied unable to stop his lips from curling into a smile.

"It's written all over your face that you're lying." Brittany giggled making him laugh. She playfully hit him with a pillow.

"You gotta understand that I don't run the streets just to be out there. I'm out there handling business so I can afford this big house, these fast cars, the designer clothes and them diamonds. The streets is how I provide."

"I could really care less about the diamonds, cars, purses or any of the material things. Those types of things don't amaze me because they don't last forever and even if they did, I couldn't take them with me when I go. I appreciate the necklace and the watch. I really do but it doesn't impress me. You being honest, loyal and committed to me. That's what would impress me."

"So, you don't think I'm honest or loyal?" Nutso asked before his phone started ringing. "What's the demo?" He answered. He was silent for a moment before speaking.

"I'm in the middle of something right now, gang," he said to the caller, who was Binky before going silent again. "All well, I'm on my way," he said looking over at Brittany who wore a mask of disappointment on her face.

"You see what I mean?" She asked. He had proven her point.

"Don't do that, baby. Its business. I'll be right back. I promise," he told her sliding into a pair of Balmain jeans.

"Don't rush, I'm going home to sleep alone in my bed. I'm used to it by now," she replied sadly, hoping he would change his mind.

"On BPSN, stop acting like that."

"Be safe," she told him before turning over in bed and pulling the sheet up to her chin.

Nutso left home and rushed to meet Binky on D Block. One of their homies, a Traveler Vice Lord from off Chicago Ave and Trumbol named, KP opened the door to the trap for him. KP was a big, black, swole ass nigga with long dreads. Over the phone, Binky had told Nut that they had just scored big so he was anxious to see what he was talking about.

"We caught one of them hoe niggas," KP told Nutso as they walked through the house they were in.

"And?"

"We snatched his bitch ass up."

"Where he at?" Nutso asked more irritated than excited by the news. They were supposed to be murdering niggas not kidnapping them. He would only be happy if it was Mo Money who they snatched up.

"In the basement," KP said causing Nut to stop walking and look at him with a stale face.

"Lord, if y'all snatched up some lame ass nigga, I'ma be mad as hell, on Stone!" He snapped marching down the stairs that led to the basement.

When he made it down the stairs, his frown flipped into a wicked grin when he saw the young man who was duct taped to a chair in the middle of the basement.

"Lil Rodney, what's word, Solid?" He asked Lil Rodney while walking circles around him. "How the fuck you get caught?" Nutso asked knowing he couldn't respond because he was gagged.

"How you wanna do it?" Binky asked Nutso coming down the stairs smoking a thick exotic stuffed wood.

"Let's have some fun and make Mo Money mad," Nutso said coming out of his Versace crew neck. He looked over at KP, who resembled the Crip nigga, Tookie Williams.

"Aye, Lord you might wanna take off that jewelry and shit," he told him while removing his own diamond chains and his watch before sitting it all on the washing machine that sat nearby. Once he removed all of his valuables, he cocked back and swung on Lil Rodney with all of his might. The punch was so powerful that it almost knocked the chair over. KP joined him and they started brutally beating Lil Rodney. Soon after Binky and Mck Reese joined in on the action. They went to work beating him viciously.

***

Hot Rod and B Moe sat in their trap on 105th with two thots that they were entertaining for the night. They had been smoking and drinking ever since they came from taking the hoes to a steakhouse Downtown.

"Let's go lay down, baby," one of the women told B Moe before giving him that look that said she was ready to eat dick. She placed a soft kiss on his neck that threw him off.

"First off, don't put yo' mufucking lips on me," he told her with a frown. "Secondly, what we need to go lay down for?" He asked her.

"I want some alone time."

"For?" he asked and instead of responding out loud she whispered in his ear.

Whatever she was saying had to be interesting because he started smiling from ear to ear. "We can do that right here. What you shy or something?" He asked.

"No," she replied. The Patron Anejo gave her a boost of courage.

"So, why do we need to go in the other room? I want yo' buddy to watch me fuck the shit out of you so she can see what she got coming right after you."

"Boy, I'm not fucking you," the friend said screwing her face up. She was an amazon who looked like the singer Ashanti in the face and Megan Thee Stallion by the body.

"How come you not?" Hot Rod asked her

"Because I'm with you. This not that type of party."

"You not my bitch. We not dating. If you not doing both of us, then you can slide," Hot Rod told her looking into her eyes.

"Come on Kia, we gone," she said grabbing her Prada jacket. She had the upmost respect for herself and she wouldn't demoralize herself to please a man that she barely knew.

"I'm staying," Kia said, letting Hot Rod and B Moe know that she was all in.

"You a thirsty, trifling ass bitch," the friend, who's name was Tamia, said heading for the door only to stop when she heard a barrage of gunshots going off. Whoever was shooting had to have a thirty-shot clip or a drum because it seemed like the shots wouldn't stop.

"What's the hold up?" Hot Rod asked her, noticing how hesitant she was after hearing the gunshots.

"They out there shooting," she replied.

"Fuck that mean?" He shot back.

"Boy, I'm not trying to get killed."

"You not tryna fuck either, so you gotta slide."

"Really, Kia? You just not gon' say nothing?" Tamia asked, staring at her fake ass friend.

"This bitch don't run shit. She can slide too," B Moe snorted just as someone rushed through the backdoor. He quickly upped the Sig Sauer that rested on his waist.

"Who the fuck is that?" He asked, jumping off the couch, heading toward the kitchen with his gun aimed When he got to the kitchen, he was surprised to see Powder slumped over the kitchen's counter, breathing erratically. "What's wrong cuz?" He asked rushing to his side. His heart was beating a mile a minute thinking that one of the Foes had did something to him.

"Shit, I'm good," Powder replied trying to catch his breath.

"Why you all out of breath and shit?"

"I just smoked a mufuckca."

"Who?"

"One of the Foes that they had working in the trap before," he said causing Hot Rod, who had walked in on the conversation, to drop his head. He was hoping that Powder hadn't just fucked up everything that he had going on.

"Why would you do that, gang?" He asked but continued speaking before Powder could answer. "I really need for you to help me understand why the fuck would you go and do some dumb, goofy ass shit like that," he said unable to contain his anger.

"Because gang, I know it was them niggas who came in here and killed folks nem. I lost my blood that day and I'm not going for that shit."

"You stupid as hell!" B Moe gruffed before wrapping his hands around Powder's neck, choking him out like Homer Simpson used to do Bart. "What if somebody saw yo' dumb ass?" He asked before slamming him on the floor.

"He was by himself and wasn't nobody outside at all," Powder said getting up.

"It's fucked up that you would pull a stunt like that without talking to us first. We on they shit. They could have this bitch surrounded right now and not just that, but this where we getting money at. Why would you jeopardize our money like that?" Hot Rod asked.

"I wasn't even thinking like—"

"That's the problem. You ain't never thinking!" B Moe snapped.

"Look, we gon' let Nu Nu nem hold this bitch down for a few days until I see where Foe nem heads at," Hot Rod said.

"So, I'm not gon' be able to check no paper?" Powder asked with a frown. He was upset that they didn't see things his way. To him, it seemed like they were on Reesie's side.

"Hell naw, you shoulda thought about that before you did that dumb ass shit," B Moe gruffed. He was fed up with him at the moment.

"Let's slide before Twelve be all thru this bitch," Hot Rod suggested. He left by himself while B Moe took Powder and the two women with him.

For the next few days, Hot Rod stayed in the house with Kailyn and Mekiyah. Both of his favorite girls were enjoying the time and attention that he was showering them with. He hadn't heard from Reesie so he figured that Powder must've handled his business properly without getting seen.

"You know I love you, don't you?" Hot Rod asked Mekiyah. They were in her room laying on the floor coloring together.

"Yes daddy, and I love you too," she replied not looking up from her coloring book.

"How much?"

"This much," Mekiayh said dropping her crayon and spreading her little arms as far as they could go. "Daddy, where were you for all that time? Mommy said that you were on vacation," she said.

Hot Rod was silent for a moment while he pondered on what response he should give his daughter. "Baby I was in jail," he said, watching her pretty face frown up.

"Why?" She asked dropping her crayon.

"Because somebody did something bad and the police thought that it was me but I didn't do it. That's why they let me out," he explained.

"Were you scared in there?"

"No, but I was sad because I couldn't be with you."

"So, what about me?" Kailyn asked entering the room.

"Now, you know I was missing you too, baby."

"But he missed me more momma!" Mekiyah teased as the doorbell rang.

"I got it!" Hot Rod said getting up and going to the door. He opened the door to see Bang standing there with a blank expression on his face.

"What's up?" He asked his twin.

"You tell me," Bang replied dryly.

"Go home, lil bro," Hot Rod told his twin, sensing that he was there on some bullshit. He tried to close the door only to be stopped by Bang putting his foot in the way. He stared at Bang for a moment. His eyes were buck and red so he knew that he was high off X pills.

"Bro, you think you know what you're doing out here but you don't, G. I don't want you getting smoked for a war that you ain't got nothing to do with," Bang said causing him to frown.

"And what do you got to do with that war?"

"Me and Mo Money locked in for real and I'm rocking with him against whoever," Bang stated firmly.

"I feel the same way about Reesie," Hot Rod replied pissing his brother off.

"All well," Bang said and turned to walk off. "You got a hard head. I wanna see is it hard enough to stop a bullet?" He said over his shoulder as he walked off to his whip.

***

"Man, this goofy ass nigga ain't answered his phone in three days, G. That's not like Foe at all," Breezy said before taking a pull from the wood he held between two fingers. Him and Mo Money were riding thru the hood looking for Lil Rodney who had been MIA for a few days now.

"Yeah, lil Foe usually call me everyday. He haven't even reached out to get more work from me," Mo Money said looking through his tinted window.

"That nigga probably somewhere laid up with a eater. If he is, on Stone I'ma tell him about his self," Breezy vowed. He was truly concerned with his homie's wellbeing.

Mo Money didn't respond. He continued to stare out the window while Breezy drove. When Breezy stopped at a red light on 103rd and Cottage Grove, he looked right to see a familiar face in the car next to theirs.

"Aye, this Bang twin driving this Audi next to us. That nigga fuck with Reesie nem," he informed Breezy while glaring over at Hot Rod who couldn't see him due to the tints they were behind.

"On Stone, I didn't even know that Bang had a twin. Fuck him, doe. Blow his bitch ass down," Breezy replied mad that he was the one driving so he wouldn't be able to participate in the shooting.

Instead of shooting, Mo Money dropped his window and waved his hand until he caught Hot Rod's attention. Once he did, he motioned for him to lower his window.

"This not yo' smoke, bro. We not into it," Mo Money told him.

"I'm not yo' mufucking bro," Hot Rod spat with a frown. "And it ain't shit for us to talk about."

"I'm not gon' keep letting you slide," Mo Money warned.

"Say less," Hot Rod replied and screeched off as the light turned green.

"Man, you shoulda just clapped his tough ass, on Stone," Breezy said. He wished he was the one in the passenger's seat. He would've dumped thirty in Hot Rod's car. He was anxious to buss his gun and let off some steam.

Before Mo Money could respond, his phone started ringing. "What's up?" He answered for Deja.

"Where you at?" She asked.

"In traffic."

"When will you be home?"

"A lil later. Why, what's up?"

"I just wanted to know when I'll be able to lay in your arms. I'm feeling real nasty right now," she purred seductively.

"Well, make sure you keep that energy. I won't keep you waiting for long."

"Okay, Daddy."

"Love you," Mo Money said before disconnecting the call.

***

Ashley was in her home alone, watching some drama series on HBO when she heard someone beating on her front door.

"Who is it?" She screamed, making her way to the door

"FBI! OPEN UP!" A voice yelled back causing her stomach to drop.

"Yes?" She asked, opening the door to see a whole team of agents.

"We have a search warrant," the lead agent who was a husky, baldhead black guy said, waving the paper in the air.

"They already searched my home and interrogated me for the murder. Now, I'm starting to feel like y'all harassing me," Ashley said visibly bothered.

"We're not here concerning a murder. We got a tip that you had something to do with the bank robbery and murder that happened at the bank that you work at," the agent explained stepping into her home.

"She was now visibly shaken up but she tried to hold her composure.

"Can I please get dressed?" She asked. She only had on a silk robe over her bra and panties.

"Yes, but she has to go with you," the agent said pointing to a female agent, who escorted Ashley to her bedroom.

For the following hour, the FBI agents searched hard, tearing her house to shreds. She wasn't really worried too much because she knew that there wasn't anything there that they could find and tie her to any crime. That all changed when a short Hispanic agent entered the living room of the house, where Ashley was sitting on her couch surrounded by agents, holding a plastic bag.

"I found this in the backyard," he told the lead agent handing him the bag.

He went in the bag and pulled out its contents which were a couple wads of hundred- and fifty-dollar bills.

"What's this?" The lead agent asked Ashley, who was shocked, and it showed all in her face.

"I-I don't k-know," she stammered.

"It looks like fresh bills. Why would fresh bills be in your backyard tied up in a bag?"

"I don't know," she repeated. She was so scared that that was all she could say. "You know that if these bills come back as the ones stolen from the bank, you're gonna have a lot of explaining to do."

"I didn't have anything to do with that."

"We'll see but until then, you're coming with us," the agent said before reading her her Miranda rights and cuffing her up.

"I need to make a call," Ashley said starting to cry.

"You'll be able to do all of that once you're processed in," he said causing her to drop her head and sob.

***

Breezy was riding around in his striker plated Hellcat Dodge Challenger serving fiends when he noticed a car that he knew was Lil Rodney's parked on 96th and Michigan.

"I found his cake ass," he said to himself smirking. He parked behind Lil Rodney's car and was excited when he seen that someone was sitting in the car. "I'm 'bout to beat yo' bitch ass, on Stone!" He joked playfully while approaching the car. His smile quickly faded into a scowl when he noticed that it was indeed Lil Rodney sitting in the driver's seat of his car but he was beat badly. His face was disfigured and it was blood everywhere.

"What the fuck?" Breezy yelled snatching the car door open. "What happened, Foe?" He asked an unresponsive Lil Rodney. He shook his shoulder trying to wake him up but to no avail so he called 9-1-1.

When the paramedics arrived, they pronounced Lil Rodney dead on the scene. Breezy was numb. He didn't even feel the tears that were rolling down his face. He had so many questions that he wanted to ask that only Rodney could answer. How was he going to tell his mother that her only child was dead? How was he going to tell Rodney's baby mother that her son's father was gone? He was feeling empty and dizzy.

"Are you okay, sir?" A paramedic asked seeing him bend over and vomit.

"I'm good," Breezy lied wiping his mouth with the back of his hand. "Fuck!" He cursed before pulling out his phone and calling Mo Money.

"Yooo," he answered.

"They killed Lil Rodney," Breezy told him in a hushed tone. He wasn't trying to be quiet. It was just hard for him to get the words out.

"Damn, what happened?" Mo Money replied after a moment of silence

"I don't know but whoever it was that caught up with him they beat him to death. I found him on 96th and Michigan. We gotta find out who did this shit, on Stone," Breezy said. He was crying again.

"Until we find out for sure, we just gon' fuck everybody up. You know how I'm coming."

"Say less. I love you, Law. Stay dangerous. I'm 'bout to get up with bro family and then I'ma pull up on you."

"All well, Law. I love you too, gang," Mo Money replied before hanging up. He hid it well, but he was also crying. He hated that Lil Rodney had gotten caught lacking.

After getting off the phone with Breezy, he decided to take a nap only to be awakened by a phone call from somebody in the Feds. He answered and listened to the automated voice speak until it asked if he would accept a call from Ashley.

"Hello?" he answered quietly. He had butterflies fluttering thru his stomach.

"Dre, they locked me up!" Ashley exclaimed. He could hear it in her voice that she was crying.

"For what?"

"They came and searched my house again because they said they got a tip that I was involved in that bank robbery and while they were searching, they found a plastic bag full of money in my backyard and now I'm being charged with the robbery. They saying I might get charged with murder."

"So, why are you calling me?" Mo Money asked suspiciously. He hoped she wasn't on no rat shit.

"What the fuck do you mean why am I calling you?" Ashley shrieked.

"You tweaking, G. What did you tell the police?"

"Nothing."

"Aight, don't talk. I'ma send you a lawyer," Mo Money told her and it got awkwardly silent for a moment. "Aye, where did that money come from?" He asked. He didn't want to ask her the question over a fed call but his curiosity got the best of him.

"I don't know, Dre. I promise I don't know," Ashley replied honestly but a part of him didn't believe her. The bank money had to come from somewhere so he was now thinking that she tried to be slick and put some to the side for herself.

"Aight man, be cool and don't talk about nothing to nobody," Mo Money told her before the call ended.

He immediately started to panic. He rushed to his closet where he knew he had two bags full of money. Everything looked untouched so he instantly started thinking that maybe his theory was right and she had put some money to the side for herself and if she did, then getting caught with it was just karma. He sat on his bed staring at the bags of money contemplating the situation until Deja walked into the room with a huge smile on her face.

"What's going on, baby?" She asked noticing the frustration that was written all over Mo Money's face.

"Nothing," he replied flatly.

"Don't tell me nothing when I know it's something bothering you, daddy," she said taking a seat on his lap. "Now, tell me what's wrong," she said with a smile.

"They just found Lil Rodney dead."

"I'm sorry to hear that, daddy. What else is on your mind?"

"One of my people got locked up for some goofy ass shit. Other than that, I'm well, baby. Thanks for asking."

"Who got locked up?"

"Nobody baby," Mo Money said with what Deja felt like was a hint of sadness in his voice.

"You can talk to me, baby. That's what I'm here for," she assured him before placing a soft kiss on his forehead.

"It ain't shit major, baby. Everything all well."

"What's all this?" She asked, pointing towards the bags of money.

"I had to make sure this count was right. Get up so I can put that shit up," Mo Money said before getting up and putting the bags in their bedroom's closet. "I holla'd at Nut not too long ago," he told her after putting the bags up.

"About what?" She asked. She didn't like Nutso too much. At one point she did, but that seemed like a lifetime ago.

"I was telling him to drop all that mad man shit, and leave this petty ass beef alone."

"And what he say?"

"He wasn't tryna hear that shit," Mo Money said with a chuckle.

"So, now what?"

"I'm not tryna smoke my lil cousin," he admitted honestly. "I got bigger fish to fry so I'ma stay out his way until he get over that shit," he added. He was still mad about Nut killing Precious and not telling him about it but he wasn't as mad as he initially was. He had acted out of emotions mixed with impulsiveness when he pulled the plug on him. He was happy that the machine wasn't keeping him alive because he wouldn't have been able to live with himself knowing that he killed his cousin over a bitch. Even doe she wasn't just any bitch, she was still a bitch. Unbeknownst to anyone else, the streets were starting to take a toll on him.

He was tired of taking lives, tired of having to watch his back, tired of taking losses, tired of all the pain that came with being in the streets. He was tired of the hood cycle that so many black men throughout America fell victim to.

"You need to leave all that street shit alone so you can give all your focus to our family. We got enough money to move to another state and start fresh."

"That sound good, don't it?" Mo Money asked Deja approaching where she was seated on the bed, pushing her backwards and climbing on top of her.

"Yes, it does," she replied with a smile.

"We can run away, get married and have a whole bunch of kids. How that sound?"

"Sounds like a master plan to me," she replied leaning forward and giving him a kiss on the lips.

"I think that's what we should do as soon as I tie up a few loose ends," he replied before leaning in and kissing and biting on her neck.

"And how long will that take?" She asked in between moans.

"Not long, baby."

"You promise?"

"I promise," he said before pulling her leggings off. The two lovers fucked for a hour but they made it seem like it lasted an eternity. Seconds turned into hours when they were pleasing each other. After their sex session, they took a shower together before laying up and planning their escape.

Chapter 9
Foes and Moes

Reesie sat in his Benz truck sipping Lean as he listened to one of the lil Foes tell him what he'd seen the other night.

"It was Racks, Mike Mike and Rock Solid. They were riding around in a silver 300C. I tried to bail in with them, but they said they was on something. I thought they was about to go slide because they was all dressed in black," the guy known as Ray Ray explained.

"What that gotta do with them hitting the spot?" Reesie asked lost.

"I think it was them."

"Fuck what you think. What do you know?"

"I didn't witness shit so I don't know nothing but Foe nem looked like they was on bullshit."

"Fuck what it looked like they was on. You just wasted my mufucking time. I should have Foe nem beat yo' ass. Get the fuck outta my truck!" Reesie snapped on Ray Ray. He needed some solid evidence on who hit Hot Rod's spot. He pulled out his iPhone and Facetimed Racks.

"Where you at, Foe?" He asked when he answered. "Aight, stay right there. I'm about to pull up," he told Racks after a few seconds of listening.

About twenty-five minutes later, Reesie was pulling up to Olivia's a restaurant in Dolton. He entered and saw Racks sitting in a booth with two beautiful women.

"What's up, Foe Buddy?" Racks asked him, reaching out to shake up Four Corner Hustler with him.

"Shit, you still haven't heard shit about that shit that happened on Corliss?"

"Hell naw," Racks replied shaking his head. "But fuck dude nem," he spat before taking a bite off his double cheeseburger.

"It's crazy how ain't nobody heard nothing about that shit."

"Whoever did that shit must've did it the right way."

"Where was you at when that shit happened?" Reesie asked and Racks twisted his face up.

"I think I was with Baby or Cello. I can't remember."

"You wasn't with Cello because he was with me," Reesie said. "Did you have something to do with that shit, Foe?" He asked seriously.

Racks stared at him for a moment trying to see if he was joking or not. "You serious?" He asked.

"Do it look like I'm joking?"

"Naw, Foe Buddy," Racks scoffed with an irritated chuckle. "I ain't have nothing to do with that shit."

"I hope that's true," Reesie said getting up from the table and leaving out the restaurant.

Unbeknownst to him, Racks was seething with anger due to the fact that he didn't like how he was playing detective for some niggas that weren't even from the hood. He was carrying it like Hot Rod was his blood or one of their day ones.

"Y'all ready to slide?" Racks asked his lady friends. He was too mad to finish his meal. The women said yes, and he dropped a hundred dollar bill on the table before leaving the restaurant.

Nutso, Binky and Arab rode thru The 100's looking for Mo Money. They had been hitting blocks for well over an hour and were starting to feel like they were on a blank mission until they saw a dark blue ST Dodge Charger parked on 103rd Place. Binky pointed out the car because of the bullet holes in the trunk of the car. He had gotten into a shootout with Mo Money and Breezy and hit the back of the car a week or two ago.

"We got his hoe ass now," Nutso said tightening his grip on the Glock 27 he held. They hit the block and saw Mo Money and another guy exiting a house right off the corner of the block. Arab stopped the car and hopped out the driver's seat.

Mo Money, who was always on alert, recognized him instantly.

"Arab, what's the demo, Law?" He yelled throwing his arms up. He started heading for the car Arab was in until the passenger's door opened and he got a glimpse of the passenger's face. Arab noticed the look on his face and started shooting at him. The guy who was with Mo Money didn't hesitate to up his Glock and return fire. Mo Money, however was caught off guard. He ducked and ran for cover behind a parked car. When he was secure, he upped his Glock, reached his hand over the hood of the car he was hiding behind and returned fire. Binky hopped out shooting at his companion. Nutso, however got out the car and cautiously moved towards where Mo Money was.

"Arab, what the fuck Moe?" Mo Money yelled only to be hushed by a flurry of gunshots. He looked over the hood and caught a glimpse of Nut creeping his way.

"Aye Lil Dav!" He yelled trying to get Lil Dav's attention. Once he looked his way, he motioned for him to take off running. *I see you bitch'* he thought to himself while watching Nutso. He didn't want to harm him but he could tell that they were trying to put him under. They even had Arab trying to get him and that part had him all thrown off.

After seeing Lil Dav take off towards Wentworth getting chased by Binky, Mo Money took a deep breath before popping up and taking off towards State Street only to get chased by Nutso. He was faster but he was getting tired. Nutso must've had a stick in his Glock because it seemed like he had been shooting forever. Mo Money made a left on State Street and bolted across 103rd Street. The shooting had stopped so he looked back to see if Nut was still pursuing him and he was surprised to see that he was. Once he made it to 103rd and Michigan, he took off down Michigan until he made it to 102nd. He went right, running down the hill. He stopped running and whipped around with his Glock pointed. Nutso tried to stop and turn around but his momentum caused him to trip over his feet and tumble to the ground. He tried to bounce right up but Mo Money was all over him.

"Cuz, what the fuck is yo' problem?" He asked aiming his gun at Nut's face. "I told you that I wasn't on that with you. I fucked up by robbing you and then pulling that plug on you but I wasn't in my right mind at the time. Now I am and I'm telling you, no, I'm begging you cuz to leave me the fuck alone," Mo Money said as Arab's car turned down 102nd Street. Mo Money took off and jetted through a gangway before Nut could even respond.

"What the fuck he was just saying?" Binky asked after jumping out of the car. He wanted to chase Mo Money down, but he knew that with the slight head start, it wasn't no catching him. If he didn't know how to do anything else, he knew how to get away.

"Nothing," Nutso replied jogging to the car. He didn't give a fuck what Mo Money was talking about. He shouldn't have tried to take his life. That was an unforgivable sin. A part of him knew that Mo Money was sincere about not wanting smoke because he just had him and one thing he knew for sure is that he didn't give any passes so if his cousin wanted him dead, he would've been dead.

Bang pulled up in front of his crib and saw a white Audi with dark tinted windows parked in his driveway. Not too many people knew where he lived so he figured that the car belonged to his twin and he had brought Mekiyah over to play with Lil Blow. He frowned up because he was still stuck on Hot Rod claiming that he was the one who killed his right-hand man, Blow. He didn't want to be around him at all until he found out the truth behind the matter. When he hopped out his car, he was surprised when Mo Money climbed out the Audi.

"Fuck you doing sitting in my driveway?" Bang asked. He was more confused as to why he was there without calling him first.

"We need to talk," Mo Money replied with a small smirk on his face. It wasn't his usual sneaky, mischievous smile though. It was a weird one. One that seemed to hide his nervousness.

Bang used his key to open the front door to his home. The living room smelled like exotic smoke and the shower was running so he figured that Alicia was in the shower. "What's up?" He asked Mo Money, taking a seat on the couch.

"Ashley got booked."

"Who the fuck is Ashley?"

"My first love. She the one that set up that bank lick for me," Mo Mopey told him and the worry immediately started showing in Bang's face.

"What she booked for?" He asked.

"They found some of the bank money at her crib."

"How the fuck she have some of the bread at her crib and we ain't even split that shit up yet?" Bang asked screwing his face up. He instantly starting thinking that Mo Money and Ashley tried to backdoor him out of some of their earnings.

"I don't know. That's what I'm tryna figure out."

"That shit crazy. How much do shorty actually know?" Bang asked and Mo Money shrugged. "Fuck you mean you don't know?"

"Shittt. She set that shit up. She was the tall bitch that Fat Shorty smacked. That's really why I clapped his fat stanking ass," Mo Money admitted with a chuckle.

"So, the dumb bitch let you rob the bank she work at and she got caught with some of the money at her crib?" Bang asked and he nodded.

"Aw, she smoked, on Stone!"

"On Stone, I was thinking the same thing. She been calling me and shit. I be wanting to block the number but then again, I wanna play her close and make sure she don't start telling," Mo Money replied as Alicia came out of the bathroom naked. From where he was seated on the couch, he could see her. When she met his gaze, she ran off to the bedroom.

"She tryna bond out but they want property."

"Her people ain't got no property to put up?"

"I gave her OG thirty-five and told her to put up her house."

"That shit crazy," Bang said before pulling out a Russian Cream Backwood and a seven of Pink Runtz. "You think that bitch thorough?" He asked as he started unraveling the wood.

"Hell yeah," Mo Money replied quickly.

Ashley was the one who taught him that 'Loyalty Is Everything'. That was their motto, so he had faith that she was loyal to him enough not to fold. He had paid for her a nice lawyer and was working hard to get her out of jail. Even though he was with Deja, and he loved her, his heart still belonged to Ashley. Even after so many years of them being apart, he was still under her spell.

"I think you should clap that bitch," Bang said, making his face drop.

"Get yo' goofy ass outta here," he replied with a frown. "You tweaking, Law. She ain't gon' say shit."

"Aight, if you think so," Bang chuckled before lighting up his wood. He hit it a few times and blew a thick cloud of smoke in the air. "On Stone, if that bitch knew anything about me, her ass was good ad dead. You wayyy better than me, Law."

"Whatever," Mo Money said getting up and stretching his short body." I can't sit here and listen to you talk about killing my baby. You really blowing me with yo' goofy ass," he said with a chuckle even though he was serious. "What you bout to get into?" "Shit, go chill with Deja and the kids. I'ma hit yo' phone if I find something else to get into." "All well," Bang said dropping a gang sign with Mo Money before he left.

***

The back of the building was packed with men and women from the OG's down to the shorties who had just jumped off the porch. A few grills were going, weed was getting passed around, bottles were popped and everyone was enjoying themselves. Everybody who was somebody was back there for their weekly softball game.

Reesie had bought everybody their own custom-made Risky Road baseball jerseys. One team's jersey color was black with 'Risky Road' in gold letters and the other team's jerseys were white with 'Risky Road' in gold letters. Reesie's jersey number was 4. He had on his white jersey with a pair of light blue Amiri jeans and a pair of all white low top Air Ones. He had on two bussdown Cuban links, one had a Double R pendant on it and the other one had a 4X pendant swinging from it. The diamonds in his bussdown Rollie shined brightly in the sunlight. He looked like he was ready to shoot a music video instead of play softball.

"Who picking the teams today?" He asked one of the older Foes named Baby.

"Racks and Bands," Baby replied after taking a pull from the thick wood he was holding.

"On the Foe lets go. Fuck we waiting on?" Vonzy said. He was Baby's nephew and just like the rest of the hood, he was ready to play ball.

Baseball was almost everybody from Risky Road's favorite sport. They all played growing up. The guys gathered together and flipped a coin to decide who would choose first between Racks and Bands. Bands won the toss. He ended up choosing Reesie, Molotti, Eye, Mylo, Wooski D, Mike Mike, Big Male and Doom Doom. Racks ended up with Cello, Lil 4, Vonzy, Baby, Thang, Shodyshod, RayRay and Fool. Everybody suited up and hit the field.

Eye was the pitcher for Bands' team. He played baseball in high school and was ranked in the top 100 during his freshman year. Even though that was over ten years ago, he still knew how to throw heat. A few onlookers were recording on Facebook and Instagram Live, asking their viewers who they thought would win. Eye struck Vonzy out before Lil 4 hit a groundball that got him to first base. RayRay batted third and hit a grounder straight to Molotti who was playing shortstop. He threw an easy double play.

Racks pitched for his team.

"You think cause you swole you can throw heat?" Reesie asked him, stepping up to the plate holding a aluminum bat. "I'm 'bout to smack yo' shit."

"You tryna put some money on the game, big mouth?" Racks asked. He was super competitive.

"On the Foe, we can."

"How much?"

"$500 a man."

"Bet," Racks said. He threw two fastballs that were way outside, but Reesie swung at both of them. "On the Foe, you weak as hell!" Racks cracked. He threw a fastball right down the middle that Reesie caught. The ball went deep left field but was caught by Shodyshod.

The game went back and forth until the seventh inning where Racks' team led by two points. Bands' team had bases loaded and Wooski D was at bat. Racks felt like he was their weakest batter next to Big Male so he tried to throw a bunch of crazy pitches hoping to make him chase and strike out swinging. He threw a low pitch that Wooski D swung at and connected. Everybody watched the ball soar so high that it almost got lost in the sun's glare. The outfielders all ran back trying to catch the ball, which landed on the other side of the gate.

"GRAND SLAM! GRAND SLAM!!!" Bands yelled rounding the bases. Everybody was cheering and laughing at the way Wooski D was running around the bases.

"That's Game!" Reesie shouted, laughing at Racks who was still standing on the mound looking stupid.

"Hell naw, we going to nine innings!" He shouted.

"No sirrr!" Bands shook his head feverishly. "You know we only play seven innings," he said.

Molotti was doing a funny little dance pointing in Racks' face.

"Stop playing with me boy!" Racks snapped, slapping his hand hard.

"On Stone, get yo' mad ass on!" Molotti snapped back. He was a few years younger than Racks. He stood 5'6, had dark brown skin with shoulder length dreads. He weighed 140 pounds soaking wet but had the heart of a lion.

"On the Foe, stop playing with me before I embarrass yo' bitch ass out here," Racks threatened, stepping in his face.

"On Stone, you gon' get embarrassed fucking with me."

"Nigga, you know what I do to Stones, so you better be cool," Racks said with an evil grin. Molotti was the younger cousin of Mo Money and Nutso. In fact, you would've sworn that him and Mo Money were brothers. They looked almost like twins. Racks felt like he would eventually end up backdooring one of the guys. He didn't care if those niggas were his blood. He felt like Molotti was supposed to be into it with them just like everybody else was but he wasn't. In fact, he still hung with them and the Moes from D Block. Racks didn't trust him or like him for that matter.

"Foe, you tweaking," Reesie said stepping up for his lil homie. He stepped in between him and Racks.

"Let you tell it, I'm always tweaking," Racks shot back. That's when he noticed that Hot Rod was standing behind Reesie like he was ready to do something.

"You always taking up for some weird ass niggas. Maybe you shoulda been a Stone."

"You saying that like it's something wrong with being a Stone," Molotti said.

"It is. This a Foe block," Racks said as a matter of factly.

"You tweaking for real now, Foe," Wooski D interjected. At first, he was going to let them figure shit out on their own but now Racks was talking like the hood was Four Corner Hustlers only. He had to speak up. "It's been Foes, Stones and GDs in the building forever. Risky Road ain't never been just Foes. Stop tryna divide the bros. That's some lame shit."

"Foe, you gon' get what you looking for if you keep playing with me," Reesie told Racks.

"I'm not worried about you or nobody else, on the Foe. Niggas know what come behind playing with me."

"And on the Foe, the same niggas you right here fronting for will tap yo' top if I gave them the word," Reesie shot back and Molotti cracked a smile because he was one of those guys. Reesie was tired of trading threats and was really ready to flex his muscle.

"Foe, you not the only nigga that's loved in the hood," Racks replied with a chuckle.

"I know. I'm just the most loved," Reesie replied cockily.

"Whatever you say, Foe," Racks said throwing his hands in the air in mock surrender before turning to Cello who was watching with a scowl on his face.

"Cello what you on, Foe? Let's jump in traffic," he said.

"We gone," Cello said, and they marched off to Racks' whip.

"What's to, Foe?" Molotti asked Reesie once Racks pulled off.

"I don't know," he shrugged. "But he gone get it together."

"That nigga weird as hell," Hot Rod commented.

"You shouldn't even be commenting on Risky bidness," Lil 4 gruffed screwing his face up at Hot Rod. He felt like he was getting way to comfortable.

"The nigga is weird. Fuck you talking about," Reesie said.

"Aight, its good for you to say that but not him." Lil 4 pointed at Hot Rod. "He not from right here. His opinion don't count for shit. I don't even—"

"Man, shut the fuck up!" Reesie told Lil 4 cutting him off.

"He said what he said, nigga," he said. Him and Lil 4 had an intense stare off that lasted a few seconds before he spoke again.

"A lot of you niggas been acting like hoes lately," he added.

"Ain't no hoe in me at all, Foe. You got me mistaken," Lil 4 replied, looking him in his eyes.

"Aight, well act like it."

"I ain't gon' let nobody speak bad about nobody from Risky Road, especially if a mufucka ain't right here to hear it. I don't know about you but that's just—"

"You act like I won't say that shit in his face," Hot Rod said.

"You probably will but anytime you do it in front of me I'ma check you."

"Nigga, you ain't check me this time."

"I'm not gon' do all the back and forth with you, on the Foe. Once it's that, mus that."

"Now that's my lil brother," Reesie said throwing his arm around Lil 4's neck. "Leave that shit alone, doe. Let's go to the G and grab a kit so we can pour up," he suggested leading them to his Benz. Hot Rod followed with a smirk on his face. Little did Lil 4 know, he had just made the list.

Chapter 10

Confessions of a Sinner

"Give me a minute and I'ma be grabbing five at a time," Hot Rod told Prince who was wrapping up bricks of coke. They were all wrapped in red plastic with his signature five-pointed star stamped on top. Hot Rod's line was building up. He had the trap on 105th, a trap on 62nd and Kimbark and he was selling weight off his phone. Reesie had hooked him up with a few niggas who were buying bricks so he was running his bag up. Prince was proud of him. He knew that he had the hustle, drive and will power to one day be the brick man. He might've sold a few bricks but he wasn't the brick man yet.

"Shit, you done ran through eight in the last two weeks. That's damn good if you ask me," Prince replied with a smile.

"Save the props for when I'm running thru eight a day."

"You'll be there. Just keep grinding."

"You heard from B Moe today?"

"Hell naw," Prince spat screwing his face up.

"Why you say it like that?"

"Because the lil nigga had the nerves to call me and tell me what he was gone do to me if I didn't give him his money back—"

"What he say he was gone do?" Hot Rod asked, cutting him off.

"First, he told me that he was gone take his money back and I told him that the last nigga that took something from me got killed before he could count it out. Then, he went off about me threatening him and said that he was gone kill me and I hung up on his goofy ass."

Hot Rod was mad that B Moe was carrying it like that after he spoke to him and told him to leave that shit alone. Prince was the closest thing to a father that Hot Rod knew and through him, he was able to form a brotherly bond with B Moe. Prince and B Moe were actually related so he didn't believe that B Moe would take anything from Prince, let alone kill him. What Hot Rod didn't know was that money could turn even the closest family members against each other. He was mature for his age but still young enough to be naive to the effect money had on men. This was his first time experiencing real money so he had to go through all the pain that came with having money to really understand. Prince, on the other hand, knew that money was truly the root of all evil. He lost plenty of friends behind money and didn't brush B Moe's comments off because he'd been robbed by a friend before in the past. It was someone real close to him and the memories of the aftermath still haunted him to this day.

"I'm 'bout to call that nigga over so we can get this shit figured out," Hot Rod said pulling out his phone but Prince waved him off.

"Don't call him. It's nothing to discuss because I'm not giving him shit. Sometime some things should just be left alone. Talking about shit doesn't always fix it. Sometimes, it makes it worse. I'ma just give him his space and he'll get over it and if not so what."

"If you say so, Unc. I just don't like that shit," Hot Rod replied. That nigga Bang been acting like a hoe lately. In his feelings because I been fuckin with Reesie.

"Who is Reesie?" Prince asked getting up, going to the kitchen sink and washing his hands before pulling out a pack of Newports, fishing one out and putting it in his mouth.

"He one of the Foes from 104th. He be into it with the nigga Mo Money."

"And what the fuck that got to do with Bang?" Prince asked after flaming up his square and taking a pull. He didn't know Mo Money personally but from what he knew about him, he knew that he was nothing but trouble. The type of guy who fit perfectly with Bang.

"Bang somehow convinced himself that he's locked in with him so he riding with him. I tried to tell the nigga that dude not right. He a fuckin snake, but he got lil bro brain so he blinded to that shit. Reesie and Mo Money from the same hood and I ain't never seen Mo Money over there. How the fuck you riding with a nigga that can't even go on his block?"

"You know yo' brother the type that can't be told nothing. He gotta learn from experience."

"Yeah, but in most cases niggas like that get killed before they learn whatever lesson was being taught. I would hate to see lil bro go out like that."

"So, be a big brother and talk to him," Prince suggested so Hot Rod pulled out his phone and Facetimed him.

When Bang answered the Facetime, he was mean mugging the camera. He had on a pair of shades so Hot Rod couldn't see his eyes. He knew that whenever he had shades on, nine times outta ten somebody was about to die.

"Aye, so when you said Don't get done like you did Blow. What you meant by that?" Bang asked the question that had been eating at him since Hot Rod said it.

"What?" Hot Rod asked caught off guard by the question.

"That day I was in traffic with Mo Money and we saw you with Reesie. When we was on facetime, you told me don't get done like I did Blow."

"I ain't call to talk about that. I called to let you know that you my lil brother and I love you to death. Fuck Mo Money, Reesie and whoever else when it comes to you. I don't like how we letting our relationships with other niggas effect our bond—"

"Fuck all that shit bro!" Bang snapped. "You said that shit like you did something to Blow. What's that about?"

"Bro, I'm tryna holla at you about some real shit and you brushing me off."

"Man, answer the question," Bang gruffed cutting him off again.

Hot Rod was trying his best to overlook his disrespect, but he was feeling himself starting to get angry, so he took a deep breath. "Bro, leave that shit alone."

"You was man enough to say that shit so be man enough to break it down."

Hot Rod stared in the camera, wondering if he should let Bang know the truth. He knew that he would be crushed but then his best friend G Ball, who Bang murdered right in his face came to mind and then he thought, *'Fuck it'.*

"I killed Blow," he confessed making Bang smile.

"Come on now, bro. Claiming other niggas bodies ain't cool. We was—"

"At the club tryna get down on Arab. I was there picking up Kailyn. I saw y'all and handled my business. You killed G Ball and I wasn't gon' be able to sleep until I got you back. I wanted to kill you but I couldn't, so I got Blow swole ass together," Hot Rod explained unable to stop his lips from spreading into a smile.

Bang took off his shades so he could see his glossy, red eyes."

On my son, I'ma shoot yo' face off when I catch up with you," he vowed before hanging up.

Prince stood there in awe. He didn't know what he was more blown away by. Hot Rod's revelation or Bang's promise. Both were deep. He could hear the pain in both brother's voices and he could also hear that they both meant what they said. He knew how hurt Hot Rod was behind G Ball's murder. The cut was so deep that it could've only been healed by an act of vengeance. He also knew how impulsive and unpredictable Bang was so he didn't take his threat lightly.

"What the fuck was that?" He asked Hot Rod before hitting his Newport.

"That nigga was getting too slick at the mouth, so I shut him up," he replied with a shrug.

"So, you was just playing with him?"

"Hell naw," Hot Rod replied with a smirk. "I did that shit and I'd do it again. Fuck Blow!"

"Y'all crazy," Prince said shaking his head. "But you gotta watch him. I know that's yo' brother and all but he sounded very serious on that phone."

"Man, Bang better sit his ass down," Hot Rod replied with a wave of his hand.

He knew that Bang wasn't gon' do shit when they bumped heads. He always made empty threats like that. He wasn't worried about shit. He paid Prince for the three and a half bricks that he came for and left.

His first stop was on 62nd and Rimbark, his hood where he gave his homie, Lil Fuller a brick to break down into dub rocks, eight balls, ounces, sixty-threes and four and a splits. Then, he dropped a brick off to Powder on 105th before making his way to Harold's Chicken to get him and his family some dinner. When he made it to the block he lived on in Oak Lawn, he rode down the block looking for anything unfamiliar. He made it his duty to learn every car that his neighbors owned so he could would notice any cars that didn't belong. A white Nissan Ultima with dark tints caught his attention. He drove past the car and decided to drive back around the block. The car could've belonged to someone who was visiting one of his neighbors. When he came back around the block, he parked his car right in front of his home. His Glock was already in his hand and with the other hand he grabbed the Harold's Chicken bag. As he was getting out of the car, something told him to look up and when he did, he saw the door to the white Nissan open up. A dread head jumped out and by time he could get off a shot, Hot Rod was unloading on him. The dread head jumped behind the hood of the Nissan and let him get off a few shots before he popped up returning fire. Hot Rod took off running towards the gangway on the side of his house. The shooter started to pursue but was held off by Hot Rod throwing wild shots behind his back while he ran through the cut. Mid way through his nice sized backyard, he noticed that the shots had ceased. He hurried to his backdoor and fumbled through his pockets looking for his keys. That's when he remembered that he had them in the Harold's bag. He quickly got them out and opened the door. Kailyn was in the front room looking out of the window. Fear was evident in her eyes. Before she could ask what happened, Hot Rod's phone dinged indicating that he had just received a text message. It was from Bang. He opened the message to see that it was just the smiling purple demon emoji. He instantly knew that it was Bang who had just shot at him. He was livid. He couldn't believe that he brung the smoke to his front door literally. The stunt was an act of war that he couldn't let slide, brother or not.

***

Mo Money and Breezy were riding in a stolen Chrysler 300C hidden behind dark tinted windows. They had been on a rampage since Lil Rodney had been found dead. They were sliding through hoods that they weren't even into it with, just trying to make everybody feel how they were feeling. When they were sliding, it was like they went into competition mode and started competing on who could do their victim the worst. After Mo Money, caught two dudes sitting in a car on 107th and Perry and smoked both of them, they were on their way to 106th and Wentworth to see if they could catch an opp to kill. After that, they planned on jumping on the Eway and riding out to Calumet City to see if they could catch a few bodies on Sibley. Mo Money's phone rang while they were riding down Wentworth.

"Hello?" he answered for the unknown number.

"Yeah, is this Mo Money?" A man asked.

"Yeah, who the fuck is this?"

"Hold on," the guy said and the line went quiet for a second. "Yeah, he on here lil cuz," the guy said.

"Dre, I been trying to call you. Why haven't you been answering?" Ashley asked. Mo Money knew her so well that he knew that she was irritated by how fast she was speaking.

"You only called once and I was in the shower. Who the fuck is this you got calling me," he asked unable to hide his jealousy.

"My cousin, Poody."

"Aw, so what they talking bout with that bond?"

"My court date next week. My lawyer told me that I should get out that day. I told him that the FBI comes to question me at least twice a week,"

That made Mo Money's heartbeat speed up. What they talking about?" He asked.

"They saying that they know I set it up and I need to tell them who the men were or else I'll go down for the robbery and the murder. They be asking stuff like was it you boyfriend or maybe a brother? Do you think you could spend the rest of your life in jail? Do you think the guy would do all this time for you? They said they got some text from my phone that's very incriminating," she said and he immediately started wondering if he had sent her any text that would incriminate himself. He planned on getting a new phone ASAP.

"Man, they just tryna scare you into admitting that you did something that you didn't do. Anytime they come talk to you tell them that you're not speaking to them without a lawyer."

"Okay," Ashley said softly. They sat on the phone quiet for a few seconds before she added. "I miss you so much."

"I miss you too my little Ostrich."

"How much?"

"Too much. I can't wait to eat that butt!" Mo Money said causing both Ashley and Poody to erupt in laughter.

"Wait until I call you so we can talk about that," she replied as the phone beeped, indicating that they had one minute left remaining on the call.

"The phone bout to hang up, bae. I'll be in the crib in about an hour. Call me then."

"Okay, I love you."

"I love you more, big head," Mo Money said before hanging up.

A few seconds later the same number was calling back.

"Yooo," he answered cooly.

"I don't know if Ashley told you about me or not, but me and her had a few conversations and I been tryna get up with you to handle some business," Poody said making him screw his face up.

"What kind of business?"

"The kind that's gon' make you a lot of money."

Mo Money's lips formed into his signature smile. "I'm listening," he said.

"Not over the phone, pull up on me."

Mo Money chuckled. "NO SIR!!" he said then laughed a little harder. He was wanted dead by many men and he wasn't going for meeting up with a nigga that he didn't even know. "Fuck I look like nigga?" He asked.

Now it was Poody's turn to laugh. "Mannnn, I'm not on shit with you."

"If I was on something with someone, I would tell them that I wasn't too. Its gon' be hard to get me, bro," Mo Money replied cockily. He felt like Poody was trying to backdoor him.

"I'm not tryna get you. I actually need you. I'll pull up on you since you don't wanna pull up on me," Poody told him.

"Aight, meet me at Gately Stadium."

"Right now?"

"Yeah," Mo Money said before hanging up.

Before pulling up to Gately stadium, he picked up Von D and Lil Dav. They were four deep, all ready to shoot something up. About twenty minutes after they pulled into Gately Stadium's parking lot, a matte grey Maserati truck pulled into the lot. Mo Money's phone rang. It was Poody.

"Hop out, I'm in this 300," he said flashing his brights. Poody hopped out of the Maserati and approached the 300C. Mo Money hopped out and met him at the trunk of the car. Poody was about 5'9 with light brown skin and deep waves in his head.

"What's the demo?" Mo Money asked him eying his bussdown Cuban link. He was also wearing a plain jane Gold Audemars Piguet on his wrist.

"Mannnn, you little as hell!" He said and erupted in laughter. His laugh was so infectious that Mo Money started laughing with him. He was laughing so hard that tears were coming out of his eyes. He was doubled over holding his stomach.

"Fuck is so funny?" Mo Money gruffed. He wanted in on the joke.

"Man, the way people be talking about you, I thought you would be taller and yo' voice raspy as hell so I thought I was meeting some big, swole ass nigga," Poody said before falling into another fit of laughter

"That shit ain't even that funny."

"Aight, aight," Poody said wiping tears from his eyes. "I got a brother that's locked up outta town. They tryna lose him and its two mufuckas that's testifying on him. Its $100,000 apiece on their head."

"Outta town where and who is your brother?"

"Iowa City and my lil brother, Sincere."

"And you expect for me to do what exactly?" Mo Money asked. His eyes were darting around looking at the traffic going by. He was in the hood and hoping to catch somebody lacking.

"I want you to collect that $200,000 so my mufucking brother can come home."

"Who am I killing and who's paying me?"

"One of the guys and another nigga we was selling bricks to. They got caught up and set lil bro up to get caught with twenty bricks and I'm paying you," Poody said.

Mo Money's eyes flickered over his designer clothes and he could tell that his jewelry was real but that didn't mean he had $200,000 to pay him with."

"Where you from?" He asked more curious to who Poody was than to the job he was asking him to do.

"Jeffrey Manor, I'm one of the Lafas," Poody replied. The Lafas were a gang from the east side of the city. Their name had been ringing since the early 2000s. They were known for having money and for putting that belt on a few hoods that they were into it with. Mo Money knew of the Lafas. They weren't too far from Risky Road. It would be easy for him to do a background check on Lafa Poody and see what's to him."

"You can ask Primo about me," Poody said name dropping one of Mo Money's older homies. Primo was one of the GDs from Risky Road that Mo Money came up under. His bond with him was still super strong despite all the bullshit going on in the hood.

"I'ma holla at him. Just give me a few days to decide if I'ma do that shit or not."

"Aight, get back at me, gang,"

"All well," Mo Money said before dropping a gang sign with Poody and hopping back in his car. As soon as he got in, he was bombarded with questions about who Poody was and what he wanted. He wasn't trying to cut anyone in on that $200,000 so he made up some lie about him trying to sell him some drugs. Breezy and Lil Dav wanted to rob him. They wanted to do that as soon as they seen the diamonds in his chain glistening. Mo Money shot it down and decided to ride thru the hood, trying to catch something. Nobody was out and he wasn't in the mood to try to hit the back of the building. That was almost like a suicide mission. After hitting Sibley and catching who they thought were the opps coming out of Castaways bowling alley, Mo Money dropped everyone off and went home thinking about the $200,000 that he was more than likely going to collect.

Chapter 11
The First Fall

A week later Mo Money, Poody and Primo were at Mastro's Steakhouse discussing business over steaks. Primo had verified to him that Poody was the real deal. He was really a young, rich nigga. Primo was worth a few hundred thousand dollars so he knew a lot of other niggas who had a sack. He knew Poody personally, due to the fact that he grew up living in the Jeffrey Manor.

After kicking it with Poody a few times just to feel him out, Mo Money concluded that he was a cool ass nigga. He was humble with his bag. He wasn't loud or arrogant. He didn't act like he was better than the next man. He acted normal.

"I'ma stand on that business for you but you gotta come with me," Mo Money told Poody over a mouthful of steak. All three of them were casually dressed in designer from head to toe. The only time Mo Money dressed casual was for funerals but the restaurant had a dress code.

"I was gone drive down there with you anyway," Poody replied.

"All well but I was talking about you gotta come with me to handle the business," Mo Money replied eying him for any signs of fear.

"Aight," he replied with a shrug.

"You ain't gotta do shit just be there."

"Say less," Poody said before checking his watch. "My homie having a party at Club O. Y'all tryna go?" He asked.

"I don't fuck with the clubs," Mo Money replied quickly. He had robbed half of the city and killed the other half. He wasn't trying to get spotted in the club.

"Mannnn, let's go have some mufuckin fun," Primo chimed in. He loved going to the club.

"Hell naw. I had enough fun here," Mo Money replied shaking his head.

"We got a few sections. It's gone be the baddest bitches in our faces. No niggas," Poody assured him.

"No."

"Bro, if I'ma go with you on the move, the least you could do is hit the club with me."

"Bro, is you tryna get me killed?" He asked with a smile but was dead serious.

"Come on gang! Fuck type of question is that?"

"I catch niggas leaving out the club and either rob or kill them. Every weekend I pray I get the call that one of my opps get spotted in the club. I can't be that nigga that get caught thinking its shake that ass time. No Sir!" Mo Money said shaking his head.

"Bro, I'm not 'bout to beg your ugly, black, Mekhi Phifer off 8Mile looking ass. You coming and I'm not tryna hear shit!" Primo said causing both Mo Money and Poody to burst out laughing.

When Poody started laughing a little too hard, Mo Money hit him with a stale face.

"Get yo' Radio looking ass outta here," Mo Money told him. "Radio like French fries! Radio like football! TOUCHDOWN!" he said in a retarded voice, imitating Cuba Gooding Jr. off the movie *Radio*. He had Foody and Primo cracking up. "Man, I'm not staying in this club all night, bro. I got some shit to do later."

"Aight, we gon' get it in for a couple hours. It look like you ain't had fun in a long ass time."

"I enjoy myself when I'm sliding," Mo Money said honestly.

"That's all you think about," Primo said with a chuckle.

"I got it from you big bro," he shot back.

Before he was deep in his bag, Primo was known to put in work. They finished their meal and decided to meet back up at 11 o'clock to hit the club.

***

Nutso, Binky and KP were in the VIP section at Club O making it rain on a few thick ass bitches. It was KP's birthday and he was having his party at the club. Standing next to KP was one of his homies named, Ant Lord from off California. He was about 5'10 with short dreads and an action figure build. He wasn't a big, swole ass nigga like KP. He was slimmer and cut up. Him next to KP looked like they were someone's security instead of niggas that were checking a bag.

Nutso had on a black Louis Vuitton with a sky blue LV logo on the front, a pair of light blue Amiri jeans and a pair of Dior retro 1 Jordans. His long dreads were hanging, some slightly in his face. He had $10,000 in five dollar bills and another $10,000 in ten dollar bills. He convinced Binky, KP and Ant Lord to get their money changed up the same way. They weren't throwing singles like everyone else so all the bitches were trying to be in their section. They had unlimited bottles of Dusse, Remy, Hennessy, Moet, Ace of Spades and 1942.

All four of them was off X pills. The pill had KP sweating profusely. Their section was full of D Block members and Traveler Vice Lords from the west side. Nutso had paid the club's owner to let his homie Boothie Bucks perform before Polo G and G Herbo hit the stage. He knew that D Block was hated by damn near everybody in the 100's so he rarely played the club but him and KP made a lot of good money together. They built a bond outside of hustling so he had to pop out for him. Boothie Bucks got onstage at about 11:45 PM. He performed two songs with Binky, Nutso and Mck Reese flashing wads of money. The crowd was reacting well to Boothie's music. His vibe was infectious and he had the crowd just as hyped as he was.

"Shorty lil ass just went crazy, on Finball," KP told Nutso once the performance was over and they were back in the section.

Nutso chuckled. KP was the only person he knew that murched it on Finball and it cracked him up every time.

"Yeah, my shorty bout to be big. He got the money behind him. He really in the field and he really making good music," he said before grabbing a bottle of D'usse and lifting it to his lips.

"Make sure you stay on his ass. I can tell that he look up to you so you gotta be that big brother and guide him. Remember that you," KP jabbed a finger at him, "Set the pace," he said. He was one of those types of brothers who made sure everyone around him carried it accordingly. He believed that just like iron sharpened iron, men sharpened men. He was quick to lift his people whenever he could. He was a genuinely good guy.

"Fasho." Nutso nodded then took another gulp of D'usse. "I'ma keep him in the studio and keep him focused on the bigger picture," he vowed as a thick bitch started twerking in his face. He looked over at Binky, Boothie and Mck Reese who were holding bottles in the air, flashing the bussdown Cartier watches they wore. This was what he hustled for, so him and his peoples could enjoy themselves. He dropped a handful of ten dollar bills on the bitch before getting up to go join his brothers have fun.

***

Before going to the club, Mo Money trailed Poody to the west side of the city to pick up his homie, Wun. Wun was going to hop in with Poody but decided to jump in his black TRX Ram truck and they all trailed each other to the club, which was located in Harvey. When they got there Mo Money was surprised when they went straight to a section owned by one of Poody's rapper friends. The section was flooded with bad, exotic looking bitches. He had on a red Gucci polo shirt, a pair of blue jeans and a pair of wheat Timbs. He had a Gucci cap pulled low over his head trying to conceal his identity in the dimly lit club. He was frantically looking all over for any familiar faces.

Wun, who was a muscular, dark-skinned guy with a wavy bald fade wasted no time. He grabbed a bottle of 1942 and pulled out a brick of crispy blue faced hundreds.

"Shake that ass, Fat Ma!" He told a slim, thick bitch before light smacking her on her ass.

Mo Money looked around the section at the rapper and his buddies. They were all dressed in designer with diamonds around their necks and wrist. He was trying his best not to stare but all he could think about was how he could lay the whole section down and strip them of everything. He looked over to the section next to theirs and whoever section it was had that bitch bussing!

The bitches were acting crazy like it was a rapper over there too. He knew it couldn't have been Polo G's section because he had left the building. Curiosity had gotten the best of him because he got up from where he was seated and crept closer to the section. When he got closer he saw a cut up, fitness coach looking ass nigga with small dreads wearing a white, gold, black and red Fort Maner jogging suit, a pair of white and gold Balenciaga runners. He wore thick bussdown Cuban link around his neck and a plain jane Rose gold Sky Dweller Rolex on his wrist. He was jumping up and down to the G Herbo song that was playing. He had a bottle of Neyah champagne in his hand. He popped the cork and the champagne erupted, splashing all over Mo Money's shirt.

"Damn man!" he snapped frowning up. "Watch what you doing, goofy ass nigga!" he shouted over the music to the muscle man.

"What?" The muscle man, who was Ant Lord asked. He was about to apologize to him until he heard him screaming some tough shit.

"I said watch what the fuck you doing?" Mo Money yelled again causing a few heads to turn.

"Aye Lord, you acting like I did that shit on purpose. Nigga we lit, enjoying ourselves. Back the fuck up if you not tryna get wet," Ant Lord shot back.

Mo Money instantly. had it in his mind that the guy was getting robbed as soon as they left the club. He probably was going to shoot him too just cause he was acting tough.

"I ain't no mufucking Lord nigga," he told the guy as Poody walked up followed by a few of his guys. A big black dread head, who looked like he could bench press a school bus stepped up next to Muscle man with a mug on his face.

"What, y'all think that big swole shit supposed to scare me?" Mo Money asked returning his mug.

"What?" The big, black guy who was wearing a Black Gucci polo, a pair of black jeans and a pair of black Gucci sneakers asked. The two diamond chains he wore were glistening in the dimly lit club. He was KP.

Before Mo Money could respond, he saw Nutso step up behind the guy.

"What's up Bitch ass—" he was saying until KP threw a hard right that knocked him right out. He crumbled to the ground with a thud.

When he regained consciousness moments later, the club was going up. As he got up, he saw Ant Lord going to work on Poody, Primo and a couple more guys were jumping KP but the big fella was knocking niggas out. Wun was fighting Nutso and Binky at the same time. He looked like he was winning but Mo Money joined the fight clearing Binky with a nasty snake. After snaking Binky, he hit Ant Lord in the back of his head with an empty Neyah bottle and ran out of the club. Once he made it to his car, he hopped in and grabbed his Glock 21 with a 30-shot clip and started the car. He knew coming to the club was a bad idea and now somebody had to die.

***

After security broke the fight up Nutso, Binky, Mck Reese, Ant Lord and KP got all of their homies together to leave the club. Nut saw Mo Money running off and he knew that he wasn't running from the fight. He was running to his gun so he wanted to hurry up and get to his.

"Aye you drive, Lord," KP told his homie Rondo as they hurried out of the club into the crowded parking lot.

"Meet us in the hood!" Nutso told KP before heading towards the car. Rondo jumped in the driver's seat. KP got in the passenger's seat while Jack and Stank Lord hopped in the backseat.

***

"I'm bout to spank his big Mark Henry looking ass," Mo Money said to himself watching KP run to his car with a group of other men. He peeped Nutso and Binky amongst the crowd of men too but fuck them, he wanted the nigga who had just knocked him out. He had been knocked down by a punch but never in his life had he been knocked out. He was steaming mad. The only time he ever talked to himself was when he was mad beyond reason. He didn't give a fuck who seen him, he was about to fuck that nigga up.

Once KP got in his Range Rover, he waited until they started to pull out and crept next to them.

***

"Who the fuck was dude nem?" KP asked Nutso, who he was on Facetime with. He had his Sig .45 in his hand while watching his rearview mirror.

"The lil nigga you knocked out was my cousin, Mo Money," Nutso told him before erupting in laughter.

"Nawwwww," KP said with a chuckle. He had heard stories about the infamous Mo Money. He couldn't believe that he was the little guy that was woofing. "On Finball, his lil tough ass," he said just as shots erupted and Rondo's window shattered.

His first reaction was to shot back but he didn't want to shoot past Rondo's face and accidently shoot him. The shots seemed like they wouldn't stop but they did after Rondo crashed into a pole. KP hit his head on the dash and opened a nasty gash over his right eye. He was ready to pop Jack and Stank because neither of them attempted to shoot back. He looked back to see that both of them had gotten hit up pretty badly. Jack was dead but Stank was still gasping for air. Rondo had also gotten hit two times.

***

After emptying his clip, Mo Money screeched out of the parking lot. He heard another set of tires screeching and his heart dropped because he just knew that it was the police behind him. He checked his rearview to see a white SS Camara pursuing him. It wasn't the police, it was Binky and Mck Reese and with no bullets in his clip, he couldn't do shit but try to get away. He bobbed and weaved in and out of traffic trying to get away from them. He knew that Nut was dangerous but Binky was three times worse. The passenger's window to the Camaro dropped and Binky came out of it holding a Micro Draco with both hands. He squeezed the trigger and the Draco roared as bullets tore through his car's exterior. He ducked his head low and stomped down on the gas. No matter what he did, it was like he couldn't shake Mck Reese who was driving Binky's car. Binky wasn't just shooting wildly. He was trying to get as close as he could and let off calculated bursts of shots.

Mo Money wished he had another gun, a extra clip or something so he could return fire and get them off his ass. After emptying the Draco, Binky came out the window with a Glock and kept shooting at him. Luckily, an 18 wheeler who's driver panicked, swerved over and almost hit Binky's car. Mo Money took advantage of the situation and got away unscathed. He was pissed. He planned on going to fuck D Block up every day just to show Nut that he was done playing. If cuz wanted smoke, he was gon give him exactly what he was looking for.

Chapter 12
A Woman Scorned

Ashley walked out of the Metropolitan Correctional Center smiling from ear to ear. After month in jail. she was excited to finally be released. She didn't know how much longer she could take sitting in jail. The stress and also the pressure that the feds were putting on her had her shook. She was against Mo Money's plan from the start, but she let her loyalty to him blinded her to the obvious. The plan was dumb. One thing she couldn't put her finger on was how that money ended up at her home. She never touched or even seen any of the money from the lick so it shouldn't have been there.

A horn honking caught her attention. She looked over at a black Audi A8 with dark tinted windows. One of the windows dropped and Mo Money waved her over.

"Hey baby!" Ashley squealed after climbing into the passengers seat of the Audi. She gave him a tight hug and they kissed passionately. She missed the way his tongue tasted and didn't want to give it back.

"What's up, baby? I missed the fuck outta you," he told her with a warm smile.

"I missed you more. I thought about you every night. I knew if wasn't nobody coming to get me, you was. Thank you so much."

"You know how I'm coming for you, girl. I woulda bought two three properties and put all that shit up to get you outta there. I know how that shit feel and I hate that my baby had to experience that," he said honestly. He might've been one of the most disloyal, untrustworthy, snakish niggas out there but he didn't play about Ashley. It would never be a time where he wouldn't come through for her no matter what she needed. Whenever she called, he would drop everything and come running. She brought out the best of a man who had no good left in him.

Mo Money drove to the Congress Hotel where he already had a room waiting for them. When Ashley stepped in the room, her jaw dropped. He had a trail of rose petals on the floor leading to the bed which was covered in roses, chocolates, a Saks Fifth bag and a bottle of D'usse. The lights in the room were off and he had a few scented candles lit up.

"Welcome home, big head," he said with a smile.

Ashley didn't know what to say so she wrapped her arms around him and gave him a juicy kiss.

"I love you, Baby Dre," she told him before giving him another kiss.

"I love you too. Now, go get in the shower," he said grabbing the bottle of D'usse, smacking the top of it with the five and popping it open. He was hoping she took a quick, ten- or fifteen-minute shower but she stayed in for over thirty minutes. When she walked out of the bathroom, she was partially dry with a body towel wrapped around herself.

"Come let me see how thick you got," Mo Money told her from the bed. She approached him and dropped the towel.

"Look at you!" he said grabbing her soft ass before leaning forward and placing soft kisses all over her ass cheeks. He then instructed her to bend over and he began eating her pussy from the back. Her juices were just as sweet as he remembered. He ran his tongue across her clit rapidly before sucking her clit hard, making her moan in ecstasy. He then spread her ass cheeks and started to lick circles around her asshole. He was the only man to ever explore that part of her body and every time he put his tongue there, it made her weak in the knees. He used one hand to spread her cheeks while he tongue fucked her ass while he used his other hand to massage her clit.

Ashley's toes were curling and it was getting hard for her to stand. The pleasure that she was feeling was so intense that she wanted to cry. Her moans only gassed him up to go harder with his tongue. He switched back to eating her pussy and put a finger in her ass and in minutes, she was squirting like she never squirted before. She immediately turned around, pushed him back on the bed and unbuckled his belt and jeans. His already rock hard dick was dripping pre cum when she pulled it out of his Versace boxer briefs. She ran her tongue over the head of his dick before sucking it into her warm mouth. He grabbed the back of her head and let her do her.

"Naw, its yo' day," he said after a few seconds and got up. He positioned her on her hands and knees at the edge of the bed with her ass tooted. He stood behind her and ran the head of his dick up and down her opening. He could feel the heat radiating from her pussy. He could also feel her pussy throbbing, begging him to enter. He entered her and slowly stroked her body. In and out. In and out. She loved how he always took his time with her. He enjoyed her sex and made sure he always made it last. He grabbed and smacked her ass softly as he began to pick up his pace. He wanted to kill that pussy but he knew that she would start running if he started going too crazy.

Her natural body fragrance plus the smell of her bodywash was only turning him on more. He stopped abruptly, pulled out and went down to eat her pussy again. Then, he licked her ass a few times before coming back up. He grabbed his dick and smacked it across her pussy a few times. She loved when he did that. This time when he went back in, he put a finger in her ass and finger fucked her while fucking her until she squirted again.

"How it taste?" He asked her after putting the finger he just took out of her ass in her mouth.

"Good," she purred after sucking his finger. He then flipped her over and climbed on top of her. She wrapped her legs around his waist and he went to work. He would fuck her slow and then slam inside her pussy and then go back to fucking her slow. He made sure that she had multiple orgasms before he splashed his seed all over her walls. Before pulling out, he wrapped a hand around her throat and applied a little pressure.

"On Stone, I will kill for this pussy," he said seriously before leaning in and kissing her lips. "You better ask Dolla," he said tightening his grip and then letting her go. She wasn't shocked because she knew the minute that she gave him Dolla's addy that he was going to kill him. The look in his eyes at the moment and the edge in his voice told her that he was as serious as he could get.

After another shower, Ashley got dressed in a beautiful white Alexander McQueen dress that Mo Money bought for her. He hated dressing casual, so he wore a simple tan and white Givenchy crewneck sweater, a pair of light blue jeans with rips in the knees and a pair of low top all white Air ones. Deja, who was somewhere outside with his kids, had seen on Instagram that Ashley posted a picture saying finally free so she was constantly blowing up his phone, but he had it powered down. Normally, he would've had it on do not disturb but then the text would still be delivered to his phone, and she would know for sure that he was ignoring her.

After they both were dressed, Mo Money took Ashley to her favorite restaurant, The Grand Lux. They ordered steaks and reminisced on old times. Times when they were together and as happy as they ever been. She was by his side when he was broke, starving and gang banging. She stayed down and when he came up, he made sure he spoiled her like she deserved to be spoiled. After a few fuck ups, she found herself a new man while he was running wild in the streets.

No matter who they were with, they never let the flames of their love die down. In all honesty if Ashley wasn't calling herself being faithful to Dolla, Mo Money and Deja would've never happened. Ashley was the ruler of his heart. Always was and always will be. His loyalty to her was a contradiction of who he was but it was unconditional and undying.

***

Racks pulled into the gas station on 103rd and Cottage Grove and parked his car next to a tinted-up Chevy Malibu. The driver of the Malibu hopped out and jumped in his passengers seat.

"What's good, Foe?" The tall heavyset dread head asked him, dropping a gang sign with him.

"Shit, what's up?" Racks asked the guy, whose name was Big Lord, before reaching in his backseat and grabbing three pounds of exotic weed. Big Lord counted out $9000 and handed it to him.

"On Muggy, this shit smell good as hell," Big Lord said after smelling the weed.

"That's some gas, on the Foe," Racks told him. He had took some of his money and sent it to King Bucky, who was in Cali. Bucky sent him twenty pounds of exotic weed. He was tired of Reesie acting like he was God so he decided to open up his own lane. He was selling pounds of exotic for $3500, sometimes he would tax a goofy $4000. He only gave Big Lord a discount because he was good peoples.

"Aight, I'ma hit you up whenever I run thru this little shit," Big Lord said before jumping out clutching his blick.

Racks was about to pull off when he seen Hot Rod's Infiniti truck pulling up. The first thing that came to his mind was that he should follow him and smoke his bitch ass. He watched as a red Mustang pulled up and a short, baldheaded nigga dressed in a Balenciaga jogging suit with a pair of

Balenciaga runners hopped out the Mustang and into Hot Rod's truck. The guy had a brown paper bag in his hand. He got back out of Hot Rod's car, holding a drawstring Nike bookbag. *'I know this nigga ain't serving in the hood'* Racks thought. As Hot Rod pulled out of the lot, he was hot on his trail. He followed him to the back of the building where Reesie and a few of the younger guys were on point ready to blow him down. Somebody must have noticed his car and stopped them from shooting. Racks put his car in the park and hopped out with a scowl on his face.

"Aye boy, I don't know what the fuck you think this is but you bet not ever serve a nigga in our hood outside of that trap," he snapped on Hot Rod.

"What you crying about now, Foe?" Reesie asked Racks not wanting to be bothered with him and his goofy shit.

"I just caught this nigga serving at the G."

"So," Reesie replied with a shrug.

"Fuck you mean *so?*" Racks asked screwing his face up.

"I stamped Moe so he can serve wherever, whoever, whenever."

"Nawwwwww foe," Racks said shaking his head. "That ain't how shit work."

"Aye Hot Rod, what you on, Law?" Reesie asked, ignoring Racks.

"Shit, I got a few tickets to this Kevin Hart show at the United Center, you tryna come?" Hot Rod asked with a smirk on his face. He knew he was blowing Racks.

"It don't matter."

"Aye Solid, next time you disrespect me, it's gone be whatever its gone be," Racks said causing Reesie to frown up.

"What that mean?" He asked

"It mean exactly what the fuck I said. Next time you disrespect me, its gon' be whatever its gone be."

"Gone get yo' goofy ass out my face," Reesie gruffed angrily. Racks hit him dead in his mouth. He squared up with Racks and hit him with a long, stiff jab. Racks responded with a two piece before Molotti, who was right there watching, snaked him. Racks stumbled but recovered quickly and rushed Molotti who he was way bigger than. Before he could really take advantage of him, Mylo jumped in. It was now three against one so Racks evened the odds by upping his Glock.

"Y'all gon' jump me?" he asked, sucking blood from his bottom lip. He had his gun pointed at Molotti while Mylo had his aimed at him.

"You upping pipes now?" Reesie asked.

"Y'all just tried to roll me like I wasn't one of the guys!" Racks snapped. He was so angry that he was yelling. He really wanted to kill somebody.

"On the Foe, get the fuck from over here," Reesie told him.

"Foe, stop playing with me," he replied.

"Foe, I'm not playing. Do it look like I'm joking?" Gone head and spin before it be too late and I let somebody do something to you," Reesie said.

Racks didn't miss the threat. He wanted to argue but he was done talking. "Shorty, I'ma teach you a lesson on the Foe," he warned Molotti, who was mad that he still had him at gunpoint.

"That's my shorty. You not gon' teach him shit. Slide bro," Reesie said firmly.

Racks nodded his head, put his gun on his waist, got in his car and pulled off. He left without a word but everybody knew that he wasn't letting this slide.

***

Mo Money finally stumbled in the house a little after one in the morning. He was high, drunk and hadn't spoken to

Deja since he'd left out the house that morning. He checked his kids' room to see that they weren't there. He then went in his room expecting to see them sleeping in the bed with Deja but they weren't. She was sitting Indian style on their bed and he could see it in her face that she was pissed off. She had on a Ethika bra and panty set with her long hair pulled into a ponytail. She didn't say a word, she just mugged him. He didn't want to feed into her games so he undressed and slid in the bed like he didn't notice her.

"So, you not gon' ask where the kids at?" She asked angrily.

It amazed him how women asked the dumbest questions when they were mad. He didn't understand that at all.

"Nope, obviously they straight considering the fact that you right here looking goofy. All mad and shit," he replied while fluffing his pillow.

"Where the fuck you been at all day?" She asked addressing the issue.

He knew this was coming. He hadn't told her about Ashley getting out of jail and he wasn't. "With Bang," he lied quickly.

"Try again, bitch. I called him," Deja said before punching him in the stomach.

"Why the fuck is you calling bro phone? Is y'all fuckin or something?" Mo Money asked pretending to be mad.

"Bitch don't try to flip the script. Where were you?"

"I was with him earlier and then I hopped in traffic with Lil Dav," he lied again. He knew that she didn't know Lil Dav but she still punched him.

"Bitch, I spoke to Von and Breezy and he was with them and you don't have no other friends besides them. Where have you been?" Deja asked

"Damn, so you just calling all my friends? I'm for real, Deja. Which one of them niggas you fuckin'?"

"Where have you been!?" she yelled angrily, making him chuckle.

"I was out sliding. That's why my phone was off."

"BITCH YOU LYING!" Deja yelled. "You was with that big headed bitch, Ashley all fucking day. She been posting your black, cheating ass on her story all fucking day!" She yelled before she started hitting him in the face and head.

"Stop tweaking before I beat yo' mufucking ass!" Mo Money shouted pushing her away from him. He used the back of his hand to wipe blood from his lip. "See what you did? Yo' ass tweakin, on Stone," he added.

"Fuck you bitch. I'm 'bout to beat your ass and then go fuck Nut!" Deja yelled before jumping on him swinging her small fist. She landed a few good punches before he picked her up and slammed her on their bed.

"Bitch, you gon' do what?" He asked while straddling her

"I'ma go fuck Nut and then Reesie. I might as well give this pussy to a real nigga instead of fucking your weak, fake, lil dick ass!" Deja spat. Her words really cut him deeply because before he could catch himself, he smacked the fuck out of her.

"You wanna give this pussy up, huh?" He asked, ripping her panties off before smacking her again.

"Stop hitting me!" She cried as he pulled off his Ethika boxer briefs with fire in his eyes and blood dripping from his lip. He looked like a madman.

"Shut the fuck up bitch!" He growled, smacking her again and forcing her legs open. "You gone fuck Nut, huh?" he asked before forcefully ramming his dick in her dry pussy. He wrapped a hand around her throat and applied a little pressure while he fucked her as hard as he could.

"Dumb ass bitch," he grunted before smacking her again. Deja was in so much pain physically and emotionally that she stopped fighting. Mo Money had never put his hands on her. She had seen him mad but never on this scale. After so long her pussy went from dry to moist to soaking wet and that made him fuck her faster and harder. He grabbed her by her ponytail and flipped her over.

"You gon' go fuck that hoe ass nigga, Reesie, huh?" Mo Money asked roughly shoving her face down in the mattress. "I'm sorry," she whined before he shoved his dick in her ass unexpectedly. She howled in agony. Even though he had her face smashed in the mattress, he could hear her screaming for him to stop. He fucked her and found time to smack her a few times between strokes.

After a few minutes, he looked down and saw blood on his dick. He pulled out and saw that he had blood and a little shit on his dick.

"You nasty ass bitch," he sneered using her ripped panties to wipe his dick off. Then, he smacked her in the face with the messy panties. He was still mad he really wanted to beat her ass.

Mo Money left out the room and went to get in the shower. The hot water felt like heaven as it rained over his body. He let the water cleanse his body, closed his eyes and lathered up his towel before starting to wash up. Deja had him all out of character or maybe this was the real him.

Either was he wanted to go back and fuck her up even more. The shit she said really bothered him. He had got snaked by people who he loved and trusted the most and the scars were still fresh. For her to talk like she was ready to snake him had him feeling some type of way.

"Leave me the fuck alone please," Mo Money said when he heard the bathroom door open.

Deja didn't respond. She just pulled the shower curtain back and stepped in the shower with him. She was still crying. Neither of them spoke to each other. They washed up in silence.

"So, you really gone rape and beat me like we don't share kids?" She asked sadly.

"Stop talking to me. As a matter of fact, when you get out the shower, go pack all yo' shit and get the fuck out my house."

"Are you serious, Dre?"

"Hell yeah, hoe. Go fuck Nut or Reesie, whichever one gon' give yo' bop ass a chance. I hope they smoke yo' goofy ass," Mo Money replied harshly.

"I was mad and you know how I get when I get in my feelings. I start saying things that I don't mean just trying to get under your skin. I'm sorry,"

"Aight well, get yo' sorry ass out," he replied. She tried to wrap her arms around him but he smacked her arms away. "I'm not tryna put my hands on you again so please leave me the fuck alone," he said and stepped out the shower. He grabbed his body towel and patted himself dry before walking back to their bedroom and climbing in the bed naked. Not too long afterwards, a naked Deja entered the room and climbed in the bed next to him. He turned his back on her and listened to her cry and whimper until he fell asleep.

Chapter 13
Frenemies

Racks, Cello and Lil 4 rode around smoking exotic, looking for something to get into. Racks had been in their ear all day about how Reesie had been acting, complaining about how he thought the hood was his and everybody else fell under him. Cello agreed. He didn't like the fact that Reesie openly treated them as his lessers instead of his equals. They had all put blood, sweat and tears in for the hood and while he was away doing his time, they were the ones that kept shit going. They deserved the same respect that he felt he was entitled to.

"Then, the nigga got the shorties feeling like they really on something," Racks said. He was still mad about them jumping him.

"You gotta look at it like this. Before you left, lil bro nem wasn't outside yet," Lil 4 was saying until Racks cut him off.

"EXACTLY!" he said loudly, yelling like somebody finally understood him.

"But that don't mean that they not valid. Lil bro nem real Risky Road. They just didn't come up under you. They love and respect you through the love and respect they see us giving you. They really just met you a few years ago but they really came up under me, Cello and Foe Buddy. Of course they gone favor him over you," Lil 4 explained before hitting the smoldering wood that Cello had just handed him.

"On the Foe, I wish I was out there when that shit happened. We would've been beating all they ass," Cello scoffed raspily. "Ain't. no jumping the guys while I'm on location," he added.

"I got something for they ass," Racks promised as Cello turned up 105th and Indiana. When they rode past 106th and Indiana, they saw Nutso standing on the front porch of a grey house along with a few other guys. Racks' eyes lit up when he seen that Molotti was amongst the crowd of men. This was his opportunity to smoke him and get away with it by saying that he was at the wrong place, with the wrong people at the wrong time.

"Let me and Lil 4 out on 107th so we can walk up and fuck them up," he told Cello.

"Molotti was just right there," Lil 4 pointed out letting him know that he seen him too. He knew Racks was on some bullshit and he was trying to stop him before he did something that he couldn't take back.

"Man, fuck shorty, I'm tryna get Nut hoe ass," He halfway lied. Under normal circumstances, he would be trying to get Nut but today he was on Molotti's ass.

Cello parked on 107th Street and they hopped out. They headed towards the porch where Nut nem was standing. As they approached, Binky was pulling up in front of the house. He hopped out his car and Lil 4 ran up blowing. Racks lined Molotti up and sent a burst of shots towards him. Molotti ducked behind another nigga who was on the porch. He jumped off the porch with his Glock 19 in his hand and fired shots at Racks. Nutso and Binky were also returning fire. Racks emptied his clip and ran back to Cello's car.

"Let me see yo pipe!" he demanded. Cello tossed him his Glock and he ran back around the corner for more. Binky and Nutso were headed towards Binky's car while Molotti was heading for his Hot Car when Racks unloaded on him trying to take his head off. This time instead of shooting back, Molotti ducked and bolted through a gangway. Racks sent a few shots at Nut and Binky before taking off for the car.

***

Mo Money, Poody and Wun were staying in a hotel room in downtown Iowa City. Poody had a homie named Angelo who was out there with the two men who he needed Mo Money to kill. The plan was for Mo Money to handle the business and they were jumping right back on the road.

At around eight that night, Angelo dropped his location to Poody and him and Mo Money left out. They arrived at a huge house on the east side in less than thirty minutes. Mo Money had his long dreads braided up with the hood of his black Nike hoodie pulled over his head.

Poody had on a black Louis Vuitton skullcap and a black Louis Vuitton hoodie. Mo Money joked on him the whole ride over he was the first person he knew to dress in head to toe in designer to go kill a mufucka. Poody told Lafa Angelo to come open the front door for them. When he did, Poody put a finger to his lips indicating for him to be quiet.

"Derrick and Dave in the kitchen," Angelo whispered looking scared as hell. He was eyeballing Mo Money who had his Glock out. Mo Money nodded towards the kitchen in a *'follow me'* manner and headed for the kitchen.

Derrick and Dave were in the kitchen having a discussion about some hoes that they were both fucking. Dave was standing over the stove whipping up some work. Mo Money ran right up on Derrick who was sitting at the kitchen's table and put two bullets in the side of his head. Dave shrieked like a little bitch and tried to run but he was so scared that he tripped over his own feet. He hit the ground hard and tried to bounce right up but Mo Money was all over him. He shot him three times in the back of his head. Poody watched with a smile on his face. He liked how Mo Money handled his business.

"It's like ten bricks in this bitch and I know they got some bread somewhere in this bitch," Angelo said kinda shaken up by what just went down. Poody had only told him that he needed their location to come collect some money that Dave owed him. If he would've known that he was going to be an accessory to a double murder, he would've minded his business. The only reason he told them about the bricks and money was to make sure that he walked out with them.

"Help us find that shit," Poody told him. They all split up and searched the house for the merch. Angelo ended up being the one who found everything. Fear had him searching harder than a mufucka.

"We gone y'all!" He said, holding up the pillowcase he had stuffed with the drugs and money. He led, the way to the front door. He felt good because his boy Poody was behind him and not the grimy ass nigga he came with. As soon as he grabbed the knob to the front door, Poody upped his Glock and shot him in the back of his head. He snatched the pillowcase and him and Mo Money jetted out the house to their car which they left running.

Once inside the car, Mo Money asked him why he smoked Angelo and he said for one, he didn't trust him because he didn't know his ass like that and secondly, he had gassed him up with all that John Wick shit he had did. Poody and Angelo's big cousin were real tight and his cousin was the one who had told him that Angelo could get him close to Dave and Derrick. Them niggas were in his circle. He initially told him that he had fifty thousand for him calling the play on them, so to save fifty thousand and eliminate a potential witness, he smoked his ass. He also wanted to show Mo Money that he didn't give a fuck about getting his hands dirty too.

As soon as they made it back to the city, Mo Money had Poody drop him off at Ashley's house. He was still mad at Deja and was trying to keep his distance. The truth in all reality was that he was using his fallout with her as an excuse to be closer to Ashley. She really did hurt his feelings but not to the extent that he made it seem like. As soon as he got in the house, he hopped in the shower and climbed in the bed with Ashley, who was watching some movie on Amazon Prime.

"I think the feds sitting outside," she told him scaring the fuck out of him.

"Why you say that?" He asked thinking about the dirty gun he had on the nightstand. He knew he was supposed to dump it but he thought that since the latest murders were from Iowa, he was good for the moment. He constantly had to get rid of guns and his Glock 31 was his favorite. He didn't want to let it go at all.

"Because I was connecting my iPad up to my Wi-Fi and one of the available Wifis said Federal Surveillance."

That really scared the fuck out of him. He felt dumb as hell for even coming to her house knowing that more than likely she would be under federal surveillance. They wanted to know who the men were involved in the bank robbery and he knew they were hoping she would lead them to them. He tried to think if he had seen any weird cars sitting on her block when he came in but honestly he didn't really pay much attention.

"They probably was. Tomorrow, we gon' start looking for somewhere else to stay."

"Okay," she replied with a nod. "Do you think I'ma have to do some time?" She asked after a moment of silence.

"Naw, they found that money and that shit incriminating as hell but the lawyer I got for you said that as long as you don't say shit, that's not enough for them to find you guilty of bank robbery. For all they know, you could've stolen that money."

"If I did have to do some time, would you be there for me?"

"Of course," Mo Money answered honestly.

"Even though you felt like I wasn't there for you how you thought I should 've been?" She asked.

The only reason she was asking all of this was because of the stories that the women she was locked up with would tell her about niggas that they thought would hold them down leaving them high and dry.

"I can't say that I wouldn't be out here fuckin other women because I'm in a whole relationship but I can promise that you would never ever ever need for nothing. It wouldn't be a time I wouldn't pick up the phone for you or send you pictures and shit like that. I would be there for you how I needed you to be there for me," he said leaning over and kissing her on her forehead. "You my R.O.D. I got you forever, dude," he added and he meant every single word.

"Thank you."

"Don't thank me for loving you how I'm supposed to love you. Thank me when I do some raw shit."

"Why do you love me so much?"

Mo Money pondered his response for a second. "I don't know," he said with a shrug. "Love, real love, is a mysterious thing and I feel like if I can break down exactly why I love you, then its not as deep as I claim it is. It's so many reasons why and the feeling I get from you is indescribable. Now, I could say that I love you so much because of how you held me down through all the goofy shit I put you through. I could say because of your loyalty or yo' smile. Its a lot of shit I can say."

"Talk yo' shit then, daddy," Ashley replied with a wide smile. She was grateful to have a man who loved her the way he did. His love was truly unconditional, and she had no doubt about that. He was far from perfect, but he was perfect for her.

"Do you still plan on making me your wife?"

"Is you only asking me that because that nigga Dolla dead?" Mo Money asked raising a brow.

"No," she replied quickly. "You need to understand that sometimes we need to experience different things to be sure that we know exactly what we want and need. The more time we spent apart, the more I began to appreciate you and your love. I did love Dolla but he wasn't you. He didn't look at me the way you do. He didn't make me feel special like you do. He wasn't nothing like you."

"So, why was you with him?"

"Because he wasn't you," she answered honestly, confusing him. "With you, everything was moving so fast that it was scary. With him, it was slower. It wasn't as risky. I didn't have to worry about the whole city trying to kill him or about him not making it home at night. You being so deep in the streets is what pushed me away from you and into his arms."

"I understand that but if you love me like you say you do, then you should've been able to weather the storm with me. It can't rain forever, and this street shit don't last forever."

"With some men it do."

"Well, not with me. You know I been looking for a way out."

"No, you always acted like you was looking for a way out and you always let yourself get sucked deeper in than you were before."

"One day, I plan on closing this chapter of my life."

"Well, close it with me. Let's run away and get married," Ashley said calling his bluff.

He heard the seriousness in her voice and it almost made him cringe. He wished it was that easy and simple but it wasn't.

"It's not that simple."

"It doesn't suppose to be simple, Baby Dre and I'm ready and willing to go through all the bumps in the road with you. All I need from you is for you to put forth an effort and meet me halfway."

"I'm saying that it's not that simple for me to just walk away from everything that I got going on, not just the streets but at home too. And I'm sure you understand that."

"And how do you figure that?" Ashley asked with a slight attitude.

"Because that's the same shit you told me when I tried to get you to leave Dolla and come back to me," Mo Money said climbing out of bed and getting dressed. "You know the saying never leave the one you like for the one you love," he said and she started laughing.

"It's never leave the one you love for the one you like, dummy," she told him as a matter of factly.

"Naw," he shook his head and flashed his signature smile. "Never leave the one you like for the one you love because if you with the one you like, then obviously shit wasn't working with you and the one you love. Sometimes you just gotta let shit go."

"So, that's how you feel?"

"Naw, I love both of y'all," he replied before leaving her to think about what he'd just said.

***

"Why the fuck you bring me over here?" B Moe asked Hot Rod, frowning when they pulled up in front of Prince's house. They were still into it and he didn't want to be around his old shiesty ass if he was paying him his money.

"I needed to stop over here real quick. We gone be in and out," Hot Rod replied. He had B Moe with him for two reasons. One, him and Bang had been trading shots left and right. Bang was really on his ass so he needed an extra set of eyes and an extra gun while he was out hustling. The second reason was that he wanted to play mediator between him and Prince. They were blood and in his eyes they were way bigger than any amount of money.

"Aight, hurry up, Law," B Moe gruffed.

"Slide in with me ku," Hot Rod said opening his door. B Moe wanted to but decided against putting up a fight. He got out the car and followed him inside of Prince's house.

"What's the demo beloved?" Prince greeted Hot Rod at the front door with a smile and a handshake. While they were shaking up, B Moe brushed past them with an attitude. Prince started to check him but decided to be the bigger man.

"I need three of them thangs real quick," Hot Rod told him in a funny voice making him laugh. He had been running through bricks left and right and he was proud of his progression.

Prince left the room and re-entered holding three bricks of coke." You better test that shit and make sure he ain't whooping you," B Moe said with a snort.

"I never whooped neither one of y'all and I never would. That's on Black P Stone Nation," Prince said coming across his chest with his fist.

"Well, give me my mufucking bread back then."

"Nigga I don't owe you shit," Prince snapped turning red. "You made yo money back and then some so that should be enough for you. I don't know who the fuck you think I am but you not getting shit from me. You can get that shit out yo' fuckin head!"

"Calm down, Unc," Hot rod said trying to intervene. Shit had gotten real heated real quickly and he didn't come for all that.

"Naw, this lil nigga in my house talking about some money that he'll never see. That's the same shit that got his dumb ass daddy killed," Prince blurted. As soon as the words escaped his lips, he regretted saying them.

"Keep my pops name out yo' mouth, you old hoe ass nigga!" B Moe replied loudly. His high yellow skin was turning red and a thick vein was coming out of the middle of his forehead.

"Hoe?" Prince asked with a chuckle. "I'm far from a hoe, lil nigga and I see that you ready to find that out the hard way. I didn't mean any disrespect by what I said—"

"You said that talking crazy to you was the same shit that got my pops killed, like you had something to do with that shit," B Moe said cutting him off.

"Man leave that shit alone," Hot Rod said.

"Hell naw, I'm not leaving shit alone," B Moe told him before turning his attention back to Prince. "So, tell me what got my dumb ass daddy killed?"

Prince stood there contemplating his next words. "Yo father got killed because he was greedy and he wasn't loyal to anyone but himself," he told him honestly.

"You beating around the bush nigga. Say what's real."

"Yo father was one of the Moes from Outlaw City. He was the one who set me up and got me robbed. All because I was making more money than he was," Prince told him. He knew one day he would have to face the music and have this conversation with B Moe. He just hated that it had to be now while all this animosity was in the air.

"And then what?" B Moe asked truly interested in the story.

"I knew it was him who called the play, so I killed him," Prince stated and B Moe upped his Glock and shot him once in the neck and two times in the chest.

Hot Rod was caught off guard. All he seen was Prince crumble to the ground.

He upped his gun and lined B Moe up but he couldn't shoot. They were family.

"What the fuck did you just do?" He asked B Moe while rushing to where Prince laid on the floor, gasping for air.

"You heard what that nigga just said he killed my pops," B Moe said lifting his gun and shooting Prince in the stomach. "Fuck him!" He snarled.

Hot Rod was crying a river. Prince was the one who taught him everything he knew about the streets and about how to be a man. Prince was the one person he could always depend on and somebody he knew had only his best interest in mind.

"Fl-Flo-Fl," Prince was trying to say something but he couldn't get the words out. B Moe slipped out the front door and left Hot Rod there in fear of him trying avenge Prince. He knew how close they were. Hot Rod pulled out his phone to call the paramedics but Prince grabbed his wrist. "Flo-Flo," he said, pointing towards the ground.

"The floor?" Hot Rod asked and he nodded before pointing upstairs. Hot Rod took off upstairs looking for whatever was in the floor that Prince could've wanted. His bedroom was spotless. There wasn't anything of importance laying around on the floor. When he ran back down the stairs to let Prince know, he found him already dead.

"FUCK!" Hot Rod shouted as tears streamed from his eyes. He cried for a few minutes before he looked around the living room and saw the three bricks that he had sitting on the couch. 'Where the rest of that work at?' he thought to himself before starting to search the house looking for drugs and money, which he knew Prince had a lot of both. After a hour of searching, he had only found a few thousand dollars but no drugs. After a couple minutes of thinking, he ran back upstairs to Prince's bedroom. He got down on his hands and knees and started crawling around knocking on the wooden floor.

After a few minutes, he found a space that sounded more hollow than the rest of the floor he had been knocking on. He found a slight crack in one of the floorboards and put his fingers in and was able to move it. He lifted it up and saw something that made his heart rate increase. It was the end of a duffle bag in sight. He moved another floorboard and saw three duffle bags. He grabbed the first one, unzipped it and seen that it was full of bricks of coke. The next bag he grabbed was full of money and the third bag was also full of bricks and a few guns. He zipped all the bags back up and threw the straps over his shoulder before heading to the living room. On his way through the living room he stopped to take one last look at Prince.

"Thank you," he told him with tears dripping from his eyes and a smile on his face before leaving the house. It was crazy to him how even in death, Prince was able to bless him.

***

Reesie drove through the hood with Lil 4 in his passenger seat and Molotti in the back. Molotti had told him about how Racks had came through D Block shooting at him. At first, he chalked it up to him being with the wrong niggas at the wrong time. He knew that it was up with his cousins but then he told him how it seemed like Racks was blowing specifically at him and he expressed how he felt about it. He wanted to kill Racks. Lil 4 wasn't having it. He started to get on Molotti's ass, only to be quieted by Reesie.

"I'ma holla at Foe and get his mind together," he promised Molotti before dropping him off in the back of the building. He wanted to have a one on one with Lil 4, who he felt was his right-hand man.

"Aye, so what you think about Racks?" Reesie asked him before lighting up a thick Backwood that was stuffed with exotic.

"What you mean what I think about him?"

"Do you feel like the nigga been on some weird shit or is it just me?"

Lil 4 thought on it for a second. He fucked with Racks. That was his boy but Reesie was his big brother. Reesie made him a boss. If Racks had been the one who cuffed him, he would've been nothing but a shooter. Reesie had taught him finesse, how to hustle and how to carry himself as *'that nigga'* "I understand the shit that be having Foe mad and sometimes it just be the way he react that make shit worse than what it really is," he explained.

Reesie took a sip from his double cup. "His reactions are the main reason why I feel like that nigga been on some weird shit. All them subtle threats and him poking his chest out like he can't get touched. That's the shit that be having me blew," he said before taking another sip from his cup.

"I ain't gon' lie. Foe ain't never mentioned trying nothing crazy with you but he always talking about how he gon' catch the nigga Hot Rod and fuck him up."

"Be honest with me, Foe. Was that him who hit the trap?"

"I don't know but I could find out."

"I need for you to stand on that for me, Foe," Reesie told him while his mind was putting together a master plan of its own. If he found out that Racks had anything to do with that trap getting hit, he was going to answer for that shit.

As they drove through the hood, Reesie noticed a dark blue Acura was following them. He made a couple calls before heading for the back of the building. The back of the building was something like their impenetrable fortress. It was one way in and one way out when you were in a car and Risky Road protected the back well. The blue Acura followed them into the building's parking lot. Reesie parked in front of a crowd of his guys and hopped out with his Glock in his hand.

The Acura slowed down and the tinted, driver's window started to drop. A whole bunch of shooters were clutching, ready to dump at the slightest sign of smoke.

"Hot Rod yo' ass tweaking. I thought you was one of them hoe niggas. I shoulda known that ain't none of them niggas gangsta enough to play crazy back here," Reesie called out when he seen that Hot Rod was the driver of the car. Hot Rod mugged him then let his red eyes roll over the crowd and kept pushing with that mug plastered on his face. Reesie pulled out his phone and called him.

"What's wrong with you, Moe?" He asked him when he answered.

"What you mean?" Hot Rod asked sounding confused.

"Why you just ride through the back mugging and shit?" Reesie asked figuring that him and Racks must've bumped heads again.

Hot Rod hung up on him and immediately Facetimed him.

"Fuck is you talking about, Foe? I'm at the crib," Hot Rod said just as shots rang out. Reesie ducked and turned towards where the shots were coming from. Somebody was on Maryland dumping through the gate. He, along with a few of the bros, returned fire at the dread head who was now running back to the blue Acura.

"That was yo' homie Hot Rod snake ass!" Cello shouted angrily. "On the Foe, I knew I shoulda been smoked his hoe ass!"

"That wasn't Hot Rod," Reesie told him.

"On the Four Corner Hustler, I just saw the nigga with my own two eyes!" Cello replied. He was so mad that he couldn't help but to shout, "On the Foe, that's why I don't fuck with nobody who ain't Risky Road cause niggas do fu shit like that."

"That wasn't him. That was his twin."

"His twin?" Cello asked raspily while twisting up his face. "Why the fuck would his twin be coming through here shooting?"

"He be with Mo Money," Reesie said and Cello started laughing.

"So, you telling me that you got this goofy ass nigga over here in the mix and his twin locked in with the fucking opps?" He asked in disbelief.

Reesie was so mad that he didn't answer him. He just turned to Band and Lil 4.

"Go kill a Stone," he told them before stomping off to his truck.

Chapter 14
Federal Nightmares

"This the nigga that snaked me at the club," Mo Money told Lil Dav passing him his phone. He had stumbled across a video of the fight at the club and couldn't stop watching it. Every time he watched the big guy snake him it made him want to go catch a body. He was mad as hell that he couldn't identify him.

"That's Lord nem," Lil Dav said and seconds later he was crying laughing. No doubt at the part where KP knocked Mo Money out. You couldn't see his face just the back of his dreads but the way he fell and how he was out for the count was hilarious. He did yo' ass how big dude did dude on Players Club!" He joked, rewinding the video.

"You said that's Lord nem. You recognize any of them niggas?" Mo Money asked. He was thirsty to kill one of those swole, bodybuilder ass niggas.

"Naw but just look at what they doing with they hands," Lil Dav said pointing to a few of the men who had their right hand balled into a fist with their left hand flat on top of the right. "Them niggas TVL," he said.

Mo Money snatched his phone and called up his TVL homie named, Day Day, who was from a hood on the west side of the city known as Wicked Town. Mo Money knew him through his homie Blacky who he had did time with.

"Take it from the top," Day Day said after answering the Facetime with a smile.

"What's the word, my boy?" Mo Money asked flashing a smile. His smile was meant to be warm but it came across as sinister.

"Same shit, you know how I'm coming. What's up wit you doe? Take it from the top."

"I'm 'bout to send you a picture and tell me if you know any of these niggas," he said and then screenshotted a few still shots of KP and Ant Lord before sending them to him.

Day Day scrutinized the pictures for a while before saying, "Who am I supposed to be trying to identify?"

"The big, black nigga and the other swole ass nigga. They some TVLs."

"That's KP and Ant but this what I need to know," he said and his smile faded. "Why you calling asking about them boys like that?"

"A lil situation happened and I'm tryna find out how I can get at them," Mo Money replied honestly.

Day Day raised an eyebrow. "Keep it straight up and down with me like an arrow. What happened?" he asked.

"I'm tryna pull up and holla at them about some business," he lied.

Day Day could smell his bullshit from a mile away. KP and Ant Lord were both getting money and they hung out a lot but they weren't getting money together. They weren't even from the same hood. Ant Lord was off California and KP was off Chicago Avenue. He knew that Mo Money was on some other shit.

"What kind of business you got with them boys?" he asked.

"I'm tryna fuck one of them niggas up," Mo Money finally admitted

"Why? What happened? Take it from the top."

"I got into it with them niggas at the club."

"Man I don't condone in no bullshit against them boys. You know that," Day Day said smoothly. Every time he said *'them boys'* he was referring to the TVLs. He was a Vice Lord and he loved his nation.

"Come on now, bro, this me," Mo Money said smiling.

"Let me make a few calls and if I find something out I'll let you know," Day Day said and hung up.

"That bitch ass nigga on some Vice Lord shit!" Mo Money spat ready to go kill Day Day. He looked over to see Lil Dav looking at him with a stale face. "What?" He asked

"Fuck you mean he on some Vice Lord shit?"

"He on some Traveler Vice Lord shit. Plus, you not even Vice Lord no more nigga. You a Stone now," Mo Money joked as a text came thru his phone.

"California and Lexington," he read the text aloud to Lil Dav. "He say the nigga Ant Lord got a joint right there."

"Let's go through that bitch," he replied.

About twenty minutes later, Mo Money, Lil Dav, Bang and Breezy were in a striker plated SRT Dodge Charger on their way out west. Lil Dav had an attitude because he had to drive. It made sense doe because he was from out west so he knew how to get around better than any of them did.

When he made it to California and Lexington, they seen that it was quite a few people out there. Mo Money smiled hard as hell when he seen Ant Lord and KP standing in the midst of a crowd. He wanted to hop out but he didn't. Lil Dav hit the block and all of a sudden every nigga that was standing out there was either on the curb or close to the curb. Mo Money hopped out with his Mac in his hands and all hell broke loose. Everybody out there started shooting at him and the car.

Breezy ducked down in the backseat and aimed his Draco out the window and squeezed the trigger. He was just shooting to get some of the shooters off their ass. Lil Dav threw the car in reverse and reversed down the block. A bullet slammed through his window and hit him in his hand.

"Them bitch ass niggas just fucked us up!" Mo Money gritted holding his arm. He was so mad that he couldn't get off that he didn't even feel the pain from being shot.

"Who the fuck they into it with?" Bang asked from the backseat. He was just as mad as Mo Money was that they couldn't get off.

"The GDs off Jackson and California and a few other mufuckas," Lil Dav replied making his way to Mt. Sinai Hospital. He twisted in his seat and noticed that he had gotten shot in his side too.

"I think that bitch ass nigga, Day Day set us up," Mo Money said to himself more than to anyone else. Them niggas were on point like they were waiting for somebody to slide. He didn't care who they were into it with that wasn't the typical security. When Lil Dav pulled up to the hospital, him and Mo Money hopped out. Bang and Breezy jumped in the front seats and took off.

***

Hot Rod sat on his bed looking at the stacks of bricks that he had neatly stacked in front of his bed. Forty-seven bricks of coke and three hundred thousand dollars. That's what he got out of Prince's house. It was bittersweet. Bitter because Prince was gone behind a few dollars that he wouldn't even had missed if he paid it, and sweet because with the money and bricks that he now had, his life would change drastically. Prince always told him that one day he would make him the plug. He just never envisioned that this would be the way that he made his prophecy come true.

He hadn't spoken to B Moe since he killed Prince. A part of him wanted to kill him but then again if he was to ever stumble across the man who murdered his father, he would do exactly what he did. He couldn't blame him. It was just fucked up that it had to be Prince.

The question that he kept asking himself was if he should cut B Moe and Powder in on the bricks he found. He didn't owe them shit but he felt obligated to hit them with a little something just off the strength.

He packed ten bricks into a Bape backpack and put the rest in a duffle bag and back into his closet before leaving out. He walked out the front door with his Glock in his hand looking for any signs of his twin. He was tired of him shooting at him and vowed to really fuck him up if he sent any more shots his way. He jumped in his car with the Bape backpack draped over one shoulder. He drove to Risky Road and pulled up in the back of the building where it was bussing as usual. Reesie was sitting on the hood of his Benz sipping lean with Lil 4 and a few more of his guys when Hot Rod parked and jumped out. Everybody besides Reesie was looking at him funny.

"What's up, Moe Man?" Reesie asked sleepily. He was talking so slow and low that his words were coming out slurred. It sounded like he was mumbling.

"I got something for you, Foe," Hot Rod told him. His red eyes seemed to glow in the dark. It was something about how the moonlight gleamed off of them that made him look creepy. He took off the backpack and handed it to Reesie who unzipped it and pulled out a neatly wrapped brick.

"What's this?" He asked, examining the brick.

"Five bricks of coke."

"For what?"

"It's a token of my appreciation. I know you like getting money so let's get some fuckin money. I told you we was gon' turn this bitch to a crack block. I don't need the trap on Corliss no more. You can put some of yo' guys in that bitch."

"You sure?"

"I'm positive and whenever you run through that shit, I got whatever you need. I'm the plug now," Hot Rod stated proudly. He knew that before the other 45 bricks he had were gone, he would find a new connect. He could be grabbing thirty, forty bricks. Maybe even fifty at a time.

Reesie already knew the team of shorties he would put in the trap. He felt like Bands, Mylo and their crowd were ready to run it up. They were earning stripes as real steppers who weren't scared to get up close and personal on their man but he wanted them to experience having a bag. Out of all the lil guys, Bands was the one who he took a liking to the most. He was the closest thing to what he was at his age.

"Nigga WE in this shit together. Lil Foe nem can work the trap, you supply the work and we split the profit sixty-forty yo' way after we pay the lil bros," Reesie suggested as Cello's Porsche pulled up and him and Racks hopped out with mean mugs on their faces.

"Aye, what's to yo' twin coming through here shooting and shit?" Cello asked Hot Rod aggressively. "On the Foe, if I would've known that you goofy ass niggas fucked wit Mo Money, you would've never been coming through this bitch," He added.

Hot Rod took a deep breath trying to control his anger. He didn't know if he had pussy written on his forehead or these Risky Road niggas just thought that they were the toughest niggas in the world. He was tired of them coming at him sideways.

"Bro, I don't know who you think I am but I'm not him. I'm not no pussy ass nigga. The only reason why I haven't taught you or him," he jabbed a finger at Racks. "A lesson is because of Reesie but on my daughter, the next time any one of you niggas come at me sideways its gone be whatever its gone be," he said loud enough for everyone around them to hear. A few people had a problem with what he was saying but he was stamped by Reesie, so they thought twice before voicing their opinion.

Before Cello could reply, Lil 4 spoke up, "Aye, let me get them masks so me and Bands can stand on this business," he told Cello who went in his glove compartment and grabbed three masks. An Iron man mask, a spiderman mask and an Incredible Hulk mask. Hot Rod looked at the mask and chuckled. The Avengers were about to fuck somebody up. Racks grabbed the Iron man mask for himself and jumped in the car with Lil 4 and Bands. He wasn't missing the opportunity to shoot a mufucka down.

"On the Foe, I wish I would've known his bitch ass was back here," Racks said to himself, looking out the window at Hot Rod as they pulled off. He pulled the Iron man mask over his face to hide the frown he was wearing.

***

After a day in the hospital, Mo Money was back in the field. He had been fucking with Poody and Wun hard. Poody had him knocking niggas off left and right. Everybody who had money on their head was getting cashed in. See, Poody didn't gangbang he was just Lafa so he was loved by niggas from every gang all over the city. When you had the type of money he had, you only rubbed shoulders with the upper echelon. Niggas who felt like they were either too successful to kill or just wasn't built like that but they had enough money to get do the killing for them. He knew a bunch of people who had checks on their head and he was putting Mo Money on them.

To Mo Money, killing for money was wayyyyy better than selling drugs and even funner than robbing everybody. It was so easy. He had been catching niggas in restaurants, in traffic, at home and even one dude at his mother's house.

When he hadn't came through with any licks in a while, Bang had teased him about falling off until he took him on a hit that paid a hundred thousand for a young nigga who was terrorizing the burbs. Bang was hooked instantly.

What wasn't getting better was Mo Money's life at home. Him and Deja had been very distant. They hadn't fucked in weeks and that had never happened before. The further he pushed her away, the closer he pulled Ashley in. He was seeing her on the daily sometimes spending two or three days with her before going home.

At first Deja felt like all he needed was a little space and everything would be back to normal but now she was worried. When she spoke to him, he gave her short responses or acted like he was too tired to hold a full conversation.

One morning she decided to wake him up to some head but he opened his eyes, moved her head, turned over and went back to sleep. She got so sexually frustrated she had to buy herself a Rose vibrator and she busted it out while he laid next to her. He watched her play with herself until he dozed off. It was almost as if he was oblivious to the pain he was causing her. She had started slipping into a deep depression where she would drink wine and smoke weed all day while watching Tyler Perry movies.

"Dre, can we talk," Deja asked Mo Money who was laid in their be watching Sportscenter.

"What's up?" he asked dryly, not taking his eyes off the TV that hung off their wall.

"That's what I wanted to ask you. What's been up with you lately? I know I messed up when I said that shit about going to fuck Nut and Reesie but those were just words. Is it really that serious?" She asked sitting on their bed. Her hair was pulled into a frizzy ponytail and her eyes had dark bags underneath them. It was obvious that she was going through it.

"An angry mouth speaks what the heart is full of," Mo Money replied quoting a post that he seen on Facebook. He didn't know who made it up but it made a lot of sense to him.

"Do you really think I would go fuck your cousin or one of your opps? Be serious."

"Precious was fucking Bone and women do spiteful, trifling shit like that to hurt a nigga. I can't put shit past you."

"IM NOT PRECIOUS!!" Deja shrieked. That's when she realized that he was truly hurt behind what she said because of what he went through with his baby momma. She was fucking his best friend while he was in jail. That cut him deep. He was traumatized emotionally and was subconsciously insecure when it came to shit like that. When she said what she said, a part of him believed that that was what she wanted to do.

"You right. You not Precious at all," he replied in a way that made her start feeling some type of way.

"Dre, right now you really acting like the bitch in the relationship. I said some shit that I didn't mean and that I should've never said, and I apologized a million times but you still acting weird. What more do you want from me?" Deja asked fighting back tears.

"Nothing," he replied flatly. Not once did he take his eyes off the TV.

Deja sat there crying. After ten minutes, he was irritated so he got up and started getting dressed.

"Here go some money for you to take the kids out. I'm 'bout to slide. I'll be back," he said passing her a few hundred dollar bills.

"Can we go somewhere together? The kids barely been seeing you," Deja said hoping she could use the kids as a weapon.

"You right," Mo Money said with a smile. "They can come with me. I'll take them to Sky Zone or something and you can go get yo' hair and nails done to keep you busy while we're out."

"Why can't we all go together?"

"Because I'm not tryna be around you like that," Mo Money replied, crushing her.

Before she could respond, he left out of their room and went to get the kids dressed.

Deja couldn't move. She was literally stuck. All she could do was sit there and sob. He was all she had. She had been by his side from the moment they met and now he was treating her like this. It was unbelievable. After twenty minutes of sitting on the bed crying, she heard the front door to their home open and close. They left without even saying goodbye to her.

Before taking the kids to SkyZone, Mo Money picked up Ashley.

"Look at you!" he said smiling, admiring her petite body in a Chanel jogging suit. "Yo' lil ass tryna get thick," he told her after she climbed in his passengers seat and greeted him with a passionate kiss.

"Hey Paradise. Hey King," she greeted the kids with a wave and a big smile.

"Hey," Paradise replied with a shy wave. It was like the older she got the more she started looking like Mo Money but she could still see a lot of Precious in her.

During the ride, Mo Money noticed that a gold Toyota pickup truck had been behind him for a while. At first, he brushed it off. He hadn't gotten high all day and Ashley wouldn't let him smoke while the kids were in the car so he figured that maybe his nerves were just bad.

After another ten minutes, he was sure that he was being followed. He sped up and tried to shake his pursuers but he couldn't and he didn't want to do too much while Ashley and the kids were in the car. He figured that it couldn't have been his opps following him because they would've been trying to get on the side of his car.

Whoever was driving the pickup truck was trying to go undetected. When he saw the opportunity to stop at a red light and let the pickup truck either get behind him or next to him, he did that. Instead of pulling in the open lane next to him, the pickup truck pulled behind him at the light. Mo Money threw his car in neutral and jumped out. He looked through the windshield of the truck to see two white men staring at him with expressions that said they were caught. He nodded and jumped back into his car.

"That's the fucking Feds," he told Ashley as he pulled off. He didn't show it but he was scared shitless. He didn't know if they were simply watching Ashley or if they were on him for what could've been anything.

"How you know?" She asked looking through her rearview mirror.

"Because they been following us. I just didn't say shit because I didn't want you panicking and shit thinking the opps was on me. When I just jumped out, I looked through their windshield and I know what the fuckin feds look like," he said looking through his mirror. Just as he suspected, the feds had turned off. They had been detected so more than likely they were done for the day.

Mo Money made it to SkyZone and tried to have fun but he couldn't. Everybody in the place looked suspect to him. He was starting to feel his paranoia kick in. Halfway through their playdate, he ordered a pizza.

"So, this why I couldn't come?" A voice asked from behind him. He looked back to see Deja standing there with her face screwed up and her hands on her hips.

"No, you couldn't come because I don't wanna be around you. I told you that before I left out," He replied. He wasn't trying to treat her or be mean. He was just being honest.

"So, this bitch is really the reason why you been acting funny. I get it now," Deja said flashing a wicked smile. "You been too busy trying to run up under this bitch, the same bitch who be the reason why you spend the rest of your life in jail," she said raising her voice.

"This not the place to be tweaking," Mo Money told her calmly. His eyes were darting around the place trying to see who was watching them.

"Why do you have my kids around this bitch like y'all just one big happy ass family?" She asked wishing that she was the one at the table instead of Ashley. Jealousy filled her heart. "Dre, I swear to God on my brother's grave if you don't answer me, I'ma embarrass all of us in this bitch," Deja snapped after a moment of silence.

"On Stone, its shit like this that let me know that I can't stick around. I was trying to stick around just for the kids but that shit dead now since you wanna be messy and make scenes in public and shit," Mo Money said standing up from where he was seated at the table. "Come on Ashley," he told her before leading her out of SkyZone. Deja followed behind them screaming and cursing. All eyes were on them and that was only pissing him off even more. He spun around quickly so that he was face to face with her. "On my kids, if all these eyes weren't on us, I would shoot yo' fuckin face off. You goofy, weak ass bitch. If you keep playing with me, you gon' be exactly like Precious. Y'all gone have more in common than just being the mother of my kids," he whispered and she caught his threat clearly. The edge in his tone told her not to try him so she swallowed her words and cut her eyes at Ashley, who she blamed for everything.

***

Nutso walked into his home at 9:30 PM. Brittany had just gotten done cooking him a dinner of Salisbury steak, mashed potatoes and dinner rolls.

"What's up, bae?" he asked walking up behind her and kissing the nape of her neck.

Lately, he had been proving to her that she could come before the streets and that he was willing to change for her. The changes weren't drastic but small things like corning in at a reasonable time and spending more time with her counted for everything. The streets had been unusually nice to him lately. It'd been shots traded between D Block and Mo Money. Plus, Racks had been sliding but nobody had been getting killed.

Him and Binky had been running up their bag and enjoying living life. He couldn't even remember the last time he'd sold a bag of dope of even something as small as a few grams. His phone didn't ring for anything less than ten grams. He had a few D lines that he let the Moes work. Nobody from the hood had to pay for work. He was putting all the Stones in position where they could touch some paper. Him and Binky had even been networking with different Black Stone hoods throughout the city.

Finn Town, Rack City, NateVille, Nine-Trey, Foster Park, Terror Town, Folly, Crank Town, Chef Town and Duck Town were just a few hoods that they had locked in with. The respect and Stone love was there and the money was plentiful. Nutso was a General and he carried the title proudly.

"This shit good as hell, baby," Nutso told Brittany using his fork to shove another piece of Salisbury steak in his mouth. He was standing over the marble island eating, smacking loudly.

"Thank you," Brittany replied while making herself a plate.

"You did yo' shit with this meat."

"I know," she boasted making him erupt in laughter.

"Girl, you really gon' sit here and front yo' shit like you made the meat when I see the yellow ass box sticking out the garbage. You ain't did shit but put it in the oven!" Nutso said before falling into another fit of laughter.

"So, I still baked it to perfection. It's a technique behind that shit," she joked. "What brung you in so early?" She asked after swallowing a mouthful of potatoes.

"I was riding around serving right?" He asked and when she nodded he continued, "And out of the blue, I started thinking about that position we tried this morning and I was like fuck that I gotta go get some of that good shit right now and here I am. I'm not really feeling this dinner, I'm tryna eat you."

"Is that right?" Brittany asked, raising an eyebrow.

"On Stone."

"So, what're you waiting on?" She asked and he got up and sat her on the table.

They had passionate sex all over the kitchen. He kissed and licked all over her body before sitting her on the kitchen's table, the stove and even the floor. The only reason they stopped was because of the continuous ringing of his phone. He knew business was calling.

After a quick shower, he left back out to serve a nigga five hundred grams in Country Club Hills. When he got on the block where he was making the serve at, he rode past a tall, brown skinned woman who was having a deep conversation with two white men. One was tall, skinny with a full beard and a bald head. The other was short, husky and had a buzz cut. It was as clear as day that the men were police.

What had his attention was that the woman was Ashley. He knew her from a mile away. He parked his car, pulled out his phone and started recording her. He wished that he could hear what she was saying. The first thing that came to mind was that she was telling on Mo Money about something he'd done. He probably hit her or some crazy shit. It was no telling what he would do when he was off them pills.

Nutso sat there for twenty minutes recording until the detectives climbed into their Chevy Suburban and pulled off. Those weren't ordinary detectives either. He could tell that much after watching them for a while. He took down the address of the house Ashley went into before calling his serve and telling him to come outside.

Chapter 15

An Angel and A Snake

Mo Money walked into his home early one morning to see that the front room was messy as hell. He went to the kitchen and was disturbed to see that the kitchen was in the same condition. Dishes filled the sink, the countertops were stained with old foods and the garbage was running over. He then rushed to his kids room to see that they were sleeping peacefully.

His next stop was to his bedroom where Deja was sprawled naked across the bed. Two empty bottles of Bel Air sat on their nightstand. Mo Money tiptoed to the closet. He didn't want to wake her he wanted to get what he came for and leave but his movements made her stir in her sleep.

"It's not in there," she croaked from the bed. She knew that he was looking for the money he had stashed in the closet.

"Where my shit at?" he asked frowning. He wasn't in the mood for her games. He was trying to grab a few dollars and head back out.

"Give me some dick and I'll give it to you," she bargained, waking all the way up. She had been waiting on this moment for the last few days.

"Bitch, stop playing with me and give me my bread!" he snapped. She sat up and he could get a glimpse of her pussy which was a little fuzzy. He could tell that she hadn't shaved in a few days.

"Nope," she replied sounding like a kid. "You can't hurt me no more than you already have so beat me up, kill me, do whatever you wanna do to me but you not getting your stuff back until you fuck me."

Mo Money closed the space between them. In three steps, he was on the bed with his hand wrapped around her throat. He choked her but she didn't fight or try to break free from his grasp. He faked like he was about to slap her and she didn't even flinch. Not wanting to entertain her any longer, he let her go and began searching the house for his money. She sat on the bed smoking a wood with a bemused look on her face knowing that she had his money hid well.

After thirty minutes, he gave up. "Stop playing bitch and give me my fuckin bread. On Stone, you tweaking!" he whined.

"Fuck me," she demanded.

Mo Money stepped up and unbuckled his Balmain jeans.

She hurriedly pulled down his Ethika boxer briefs and exposed his soft dick. She then hungrily sucked his dick into her mouth and started sucking like she was trying to win a million dollars. In seconds, his dick was standing at full attention. She held it with two hands while working her magic.

"Move yo' fuckin hands," Mo Money demanded. When she did, he grabbed the back of her head and forced his dick deep down her throat. She choked and gagged but continued to suck. Tears were falling down her cheeks due to her coking so hard on his dick. He held her head steady and fucked her face. He was intentionally trying to hurt her, but little did he know she was enjoying every second.

She relaxed the muscles in her throat and put every inch of his dick inside her mouth before slowly spitting it out. She then grabbed his wet, slippery dick and lifted it up so she could suck his nuts. She did one at a time before putting his whole sack in her mouth and humming while she stroked his dick with her small hands. This was the best head she had given him in a while and she knew it. She turned over so he could hit her from the back. He slowly entered his hard dick into her throbbing pussy to feel that she was wetter than ever. It felt like she had a whole tube of lube in her pussy but that was just her natural wetness. She was craving his dick. He went in giving her long strokes that seemed to tap her soul by the way she was moaning.

"Fuck me harder, daddy," Deja purred. She needed to feel him. She wanted him to hurt her because she felt like if it hurt then it was real. He did as told and held on to her hips while he fucked the shit out of her. She cried, yelled, cursed and moaned while she tried to take the dick.

"Pull my hair!" She told him. He grabbed a handful of her hair and yanked her head back while slamming his dick deep inside he guts. Her pussy was so creamy that his black dick was painted white with her cream.

"Turn over," Mo Money commanded. When she flipped over, he grabbed her by her ankles and held her legs in the air while beating her pussy up. When she started squirting, he pulled out and started smacking her clit with his dick. The sounds of her wet pussy gushing mixed with her moans and cries only made him fuck her harder and faster. She told him to choke her, spit in her mouth and even to smack her and that shit turned him on even more.

When he nutted, he let out a animalistic grunt and kept stroking until his dick went limp while still inside of her. "Now grab that bread," he told her sliding out of her with a plop.

"Eat my ass," she told him. He didn't know if she was serious or not but he wanted his money so he flipped her over and licked her ass while fingering her pussy until she came on his fingers. "You forgot to suck my toes," she told him and he smacked his lips before flipping her over and grabbing one of her feet. He sucked her toes then switched to the other foot, sucked every toe then ran his tongue from her toes to the heel of her foot and then back up. He kissed the bottom of both feet for good measure.

"Can I have my shit now?" He asked. His dick was back rock hard.

Somehow, Someway, Deja convinced him to give her another round that lasted nearly an hour. This time the power of the pussy put him right to sleep. Deja was overwhelmed with joy as she went to sleep in his arms.

A few hours later, she woke him up to some deep throat.

"Your money right there," she told him before going back to sucking his dick.

She grabbed his hand and placed it on her ass. He took that as an invitation to stick his finger in it. That seemed like it made her suck his dick even better. In a matter of minutes, he was cumming. She swallowed every drop before tucking his dick back in his briefs.

"Daddy, if you keep playing with me, I'ma kill that big headed bitch," she said before planting a couple soft kisses on his chest.

"You ain't gon' kill shit," he chuckled before getting out of bed and getting dressed.

"On my kids, you gone see," she replied with a smile." So, when are you going to come back?"

"If you gon' suck my dick like you did earlier, then I'll be right back."

"Only if you put your tongue in my booty and let me throw it back on your face."

"Deal," Mo Money said with a smile before leaving.

After leaving, he went to pick up Breezy. He had somebody to knock off for fifty thousand and he was taking Breezy with him. Before they made it out the hood, he got a call from a unknown number.

"Yoooo," he answered.

"Hey Dre, this Tee Tee," the woman on the other end said.

"Which Tee Tee?"

"Tee Tee, Tee Tee from the building," she replied.

"Awww, what's up, Tee Tee. You straight?"

"Yeah, I was calling because my momma wanted to talk to you. Its important."

"Put her on the phone."

"I'm about to send you our location. She want you to come over."

"Well," Mo Money replied and hung up. She immediately sent him her location. He made his way that way all while wondering what the fuck her mother wanted with him. He told Breezy and he was just as clueless as he was. It took him thirty minutes to make it to Ms. Spivey's house in Olympia Fields. The home was huge. Mo Money led Breezy to the front door and rang the doorbell. Seconds later, Tee Tee swung the door open. She stood about 5'6 with dark brown skin, the sexiest juicy lips, big titties and an ass that complimented her thick thighs.

"Hey y'all!" She greeted both of them with a hug and a smile. She was a couple years older than Mo Money and had watched them grow up in the building. She led them to the living room of the home and he froze in his tracks when he seen Reesie, Lil 4 and ShodyShod sitting on the couch having a conversation with her mother, Ms. Spivey.

"Hey Dre," Ms. Spivey said with a smile. Mo Money walked over and gave her a hug. Breezy did the same. "Have a seat so we can talk."

"What's going on?" Mo Money asked knowing it had to be something important for her to have him and Reesie in the same room. The whole hood knew of their beef.

"Well, I don't know if any of you knew but my sons are on their way home," she said causing the whole room to smile. Risky and B.T had been gone since they were shorties for a home invasion and murder that they caught together. B.T and Mo Money were the same age and Risky was a year older. They were the first two in their age range that hopped off the porch. Without them, it would be no Reesie, Mo Money or Racks. They were the pioneers. Everybody from

Risky Road feared and respected Risky and B.T. They were two of the most outstanding members.

"When they get out?" Reesie asked. He was probably the most anxious one in the room. Just like everyone else from the hood he idolized Risky and B.T. He knew that they both would be proud of him and how far he had come. He couldn't wait till they got out and witnessed how he had the streets in a headlock.

"In ten days," Ms. Spivey said with a broad smile. "We' re having a welcome home party for them in the back of the buildings and they want all of you there," she said looking around the room at how all of their facial expressions changed. "They know all about whatever y'all got going on but they said they expect for y'all to act like its squashed for them for that one day. They've been gone for over ten years now and they just want to see all of their friends that still alive together. Is that too much to ask for?"

"No, "everybody said in unison. Nobody was crazy enough to go against their wishes. A lot of things had changed since Risky and B.T had been gone but one thing that didn't change was their influence over the hood.

"Are you guys sure?" Ms. Spivey asked. She remembered that Big Risky had gotten killed by the police because the same young men that were sitting with her couldn't control themselves.

"Yeah ma, you got my word," Reesie said sweetly.

"Okay, I'ma let y'all speak for a moment," she said before leading Tee Tee out of the living room.

ShodyShod was the first to speak. "Breezy you a hoe," he said in a joking manner with a smile on his face.

"What's the word, Solid?" Breezy asked. "Foe nem finally finna come home. It seem like forever since they been out here."

"Hell yeah," Reesie replied before turning his attention to Mo Money who was sitting there quietly. "We gotta let everybody know that ain't shit shaking the day Foe nem come home. Any nigga from my side or yours that send a shot or act crazy, he dead."

"Aight, that sound about right. I'ma be there and I expect for you to stand on the guys and make sure that they don't kill me back there," Mo Money replied. Reesie had influence over the hood than anyone else whereas he was something of an outlaw so if anybody was to get fucked up that day, it would most likely be him.

"On the Foe, on my brother, ain't nobody gone be on shit. That's Foe nem day and we gon' make sure foe nem' come home the right way," Reesie replied.

Mo Money knew he couldn't trust Reesie but for Risky and B.T, he would have to take the risk.

"That's what it is then," he said, extending his hand to him and for the first time since they were teenagers the two men shook up. It was fascinating how something so small as a handshake could be so colossal but it was. The love and respect they had For Risky and B.T was enough to douse the flames of their hatred for one another.

ShodyShod, who was basically neutral in the war, smiled. "So, we got one day to be on our 'Condos' shit, huh?" he asked.

'The Condos' was what their building was called before Big Risky died and they changed the name of their hood to Risky Road in honor of him. You didn't have to be from the building to be Risky Road even though the buildings was their headquarters but back in the day when they were corning up, you had to live in the building to say you were from 'The Condos'.

"On the Foe, we gotta do it big for Foe nem," Lil 4 said to no one in particular. Risky and B.T coming home was a big deal but nobody in the room knew how much they would impact the grand scheme of things in the future.

Mo Money and Bang were fresh off a lick when Mo Money got a Facetime from Nutso.

"What's the demo, cuz?"

"What's the word, cuz? Who you with?"

"Who the fuck you with nigga?" Mo Money shot back.

"I'm with the Boogeyman," Nutso said putting the camera on Binky who was high as hell off Percs with an ugly mug on his face.

"I'm with Bang. What's up, ku?"

"What's up with yo' lil bitch Ashley?"

"Fuck you mean what's up with her? Don't play with me Nut for real. On Stone, you tweaking," Mo Money said thinking that he was about to pull some bullshit.

"I saw that bitch talking to the feds, boy."

"Fuck outta here," Mo Money replied smacking his lips in disbelief.

"On BPSN," Nut said and then paused the Facetime. A few seconds later, he got a text from him. "Check that out then call me back," he said and disconnected the call.

Mo Money opened up the text to see a video. He watched the video of Ashley talking to two agents. He couldn't really make out their faces but they looked like they could've been the same agents that were following them the day they took the kids to SkyZone. His stomach instantly twisted into knots, and he felt like he had to throw up.

"Man, that bitch a rat! On Stone, I told you!" Bang scoffed angrily. He had been told him that he needed to smoke that hoe because she knew too much. Fuck the bank robbery. She knew about enough murders and other shit to get him enough time in jail to pass to his kids kids kids and then their kids.

"Naw, she told me that them people been pressing her to give up some names. They probably just pulled up tryna get her to talk," Mo Money replied unconvincingly. He could fool himself but he couldn't fool Bang. The bitch was snitching.

"Man, fuck what you talking about, Moe. You gotta smoke that bitch, on Stone!" Bang urged. "If you don't wanna do it, let me do it," he added.

"It ain't that serious, Law. She not telling," he replied with a slight attitude.

"All well, drop me off bro," Bang told him and he did just that. He didn't give a fuck about hanging with a nigga. He did better on his own.

After dropping Bang off, he wanted to confront Ashley but he didn't know how without making her feel some type of way. He didn't want to scare her plus he was scared to pull up on her not knowing if the feds would be outside her house waiting on him. He decided to go home and the look on Deja's face when he entered their bedroom made him smile. She lit up like a kid on Christmas when she seen him. It was getting late, and she was starting to think that he wasn't coming back.

"Hey, Daddy! Come here, let me suck that dick," she purred happy to see him. She planned on being as nasty as she could for him until he fully forgave her. He stood at the edge of their bed and she sucked his dick like a beast until he came in her mouth. She spit his nut over his dick and used it to smear the nut all over her lips then seductively licked it all off." I got a surprise for you daddy,"

"And what's that?" he asked kicking off his retro 7 Jordans.

She took off the Ethika boxer briefs she had on, turned around and poked her ass in the air.

"Can you see it?" she asked rubbing her clit. She was talking about the fresh tattoo that covered her ass. It said Mo on one cheek and Money on the other surrounded by a big ass butterfly. She already had his name on her wrist and his government on her foot. He admired the ink as well as her pretty pussy. She was now shoving two fingers in and out of herself and her juices were dripping down her legs.

"I miss you so much, daddy," she moaned working her fingers. He climbed behind her and tore that ass up until she was squirting everywhere. After he nutted, she rushed to get a hot, soapy towel to clean him up.

The next morning, Deja woke Mo Money up to some head and then a big breakfast. The house was clean and nice looking and Deja was looking better than she had in a long time.

"I rolled you a wood, daddy. Anything else you need me to do?" She asked politely and he started cracking up.

"Why you in this bitch actin like the maid off the Jeffersons?" He asked still laughing.

"I'm just trying to keep you happy, baby," Deja answered honestly.

"You good baby. We good," he assured her. "What you got planned for the day?"

"Nothing."

"Aight, you can hop in traffic with me if you want to."

"Okay," she said turning her head so he couldn't see the smile on her face. She silently thanked God for the sudden shift of his attitude. After they showered and got dressed, they left and went downtown to shop. Mo Money ran into Arab at the Burberry store.

"How you coming, gang?" He asked Arab matching his mug. "You always told me that you would never pick sides between me and Nut but you was with them niggas tryna get down on me," Mo Money said with a hint of sadness in his voice.

"I was gone stay out of it until Nut told me that it was you and Bang who killed my pops," he replied with venom in his voice and death in his mug.

Mo Money had a fake look of shock on his face. "How the fuck he gon' say some bullshit like that?" He asked.

"He said you called the play and opped him for Bang."

"Hell naw!" Mo Money lied quickly, vehemently shaking his head. "On Stone, cuz getting that desperate that he gotta make up shit to get help. That's crazy," he said shaking his head again this time a little calmer. He had finally figured out why Arab had been trying to get up with him so bad. He was trying to backdoor him. The constant calls trying to link, the incident on Langley, it all made perfect sense now.

"Bro, I didn't have shit to do with yo' pops getting killed and that's on the five," he lied pounding his chest. He could see himself shooting Arab all in his face. It was no way he was letting him slide for trying to get him.

"I'm just letting you know what was brought to me."

"So, now what? Do I need to be watching my back for you, too?"

"Naw, you say you didn't have nothing to do with that shit. I'ma take yo' word for it. Pardon my body for not coming at you straight up in the first place," Arab said extending his hand for a shake. They held eye contact while shaking up. Both men had treacherous thoughts running through their minds. He knew Mo Money so he knew how vindictive he was. He could hold a grudge forever and he was one of the sneakiest men he ever met. He made Judas look loyal. His smile most definitely didn't match his shake and it was crazy because he was thinking the exact same thing about him. The bond they used to share was no more. The love was gone.

"Keep yo' head up out here law," Mo Money told him.

"You too, Law. Stay dangerous."

"Fasho," Mo Money said watching him walk off. He waited a few minutes before leaving himself. He wasn't going to end his spending spree but he was damn sure getting out of the Burberry store.

Deja enjoyed herself during the shopping spree. Mo Money bought her everything she even looked like she wanted. Shoes, purses, dresses, scarves and whatever else her heart desired. This was the version of him that she missed. The guy that spoiled her rotten and treated her like she was God's gift to man.

After a shopping spree that lasted a few hours, he took her to Benihanas for a nice lunch. During lunch, she noticed that someone was blowing his phone up with text and calls. She appreciated that he didn't answer any call due to the fact that he was trying to give her his full attention. One text, a very long one, must've been disturbing because his whole mood changed.

"I gotta go handle some business after we eat so I'ma drop you off," he told her over a mouthful of fish.

"Okay," Deja replied somberly. She was having the time of her life. She would've bet her last dollar that it was that big headed bitch Ashley who was killing their vibe. They finished eating and as soon as they got in the car, en route to their house, she started sucking his dick. She was hoping that the sloppy toppy would convince him to stay with her but it didn't. He dropped her off and didn't even tell her that he loved her before he pulled off.

About thirty minutes later, Mo Money was pulling up in front of Ashley's house. He looked up and down the block before tucking his Glock, hopping out the car and scurrying into her house.

"Why the fuck do I have to keep calling and texting you? I hate when you start acting weird," Ashley snapped as soon as he crossed the threshold. She was dressed in Dolce and Gabanna from head to toe and the Dior perfume she wore was mesmerizing.

"I was busy," Mo Money said looking out of her front window. He was trying to see if he could spot any funny looking car but due to him being so paranoid, every car on the block looked suspect. He still hadn't confronted her about the video Nut had sent him.

"I need some money," she told him with an attitude.

"How much?"

"Enough to buy me a new car."

"What you need a new car for?"

"Because I think the feds know my car, so I want one of those BMWs."

"What BMW?" He asked looking at her like she was crazy.

"I don't know what it's called but it's a 2 Series."

"Fuck a new car. You should be tryna find a new house but how much do you need?"

"Just give me about fifty thousand," she said like that was nothing. She knew that he was holding and wouldn't complain about the amount.

"Dude, if you go put fifty thousand on a new car they really gon' think you had something to do with that shit you need to start thinking for you get yo'self booked," he told her pulling a wood out his hoody pocket.

"Just say you don't want to give me the money," Ashley shot back, frowning.

"You know the money ain't a problem. I just don't want you to put a real spotlight on yourself."

"Well, give me enough to put down on one to ride off the lot."

"How freaky you gone get for a new BMW?"

"As freaky as you want me to be," she replied seductively batting her eyes.

"Have you heard from yo' lawyers?"

"I got court next month for a status hearing. They said they still waiting on discovery or something like that."

"Have the police been fucking with you?"

"No," she replied quickly. "I think they be following me sometimes but that's it. They haven't been calling me or nothing," she lied reaching for the wood. The questions he was asking were making her uncomfortable. She hit the wood a few times before coughing. "I think I saw your friend the other day," she said raspily.

"Which friend?"

"The one with the red eyes that always wear the shades. What's his name?" She asked.

Mo Money knew that she was talking about Bang but he played dumb. "I don't know who you talking about," he lied.

"He was with y'all the day y'all robbed the bank," Ashley replied almost making his eyes bulge out of his head.

"I don't know what you talking about. You tweaking."

"Stop playing," Ashley said giggling.

Mo Money reached under her shirt and ran his hand over her chest before pinching one of her nipples. He was discreetly checking to see if she was wearing a wire.

"Come here," he told her. She climbed on his lap and he whispered in her ear. "Loyalty is Everything, right?" he asked and she nodded. "You know if you were to ever betray me in any way, I would kill you right? And even if I couldn't one of my people would."

"I know, Baby Dre."

Mo Money pulled his phone out and went to the video. She watched it in silence her heart was beating a mile a minute. Her palms were wet with sweat and a lump formed in her throat. She didn't know what to expect from him.

"I'ma ask you one time. Ashley, did you tell the feds that I had anything to do with that bank robbery?" He asked.

"No," she whispered, shaking her head. A few tears escaped the corner of her eyes. "They were listening to my calls while I was locked up and they were watching me as soon as I got out. They said that they know that it was you who I helped rob the bank."

"And what did you say?"

"I told them that you didn't have anything to do with it. They told me that if I told on you, I would only get a few years probation as a deal," she said and that's when she noticed the gun clinched in his hand. "Nooooo, please don't kill me, Dre," she cried.

"Don't say my fuckin name!" Mo Money gruffed in a hushed tone. He was paranoid as hell thinking that her house was bugged with audio and video. He could see it in her eyes that she wasn't keeping it one hundred with him. He could see the guilt and nervousness in her eyes. He thought about what Bang had said and decided that he had to get rid of her. "On Stone, I can't believe you," he told her sadly, pushing her off of his lap.

"Just help me give them your friend and we'll be good," she said and he put his gun to her forehead.

"Bitch, don't never suggest that I snitch on a mufucka!" he snapped, pressing the barrel into her forehead. Take all that shit off right now," he said and she complied.

She stripped naked and he was satisfied when he didn't see a wire or recording device. He wanted to kill her right then and there but his intuition told him that that was the wrong move to make.

"Is the feds outside?" he asked, peeking out the window.

"Yes," Ashley answered with a nod.

The pain in his expression was so strong that she couldn't continue to look him in his eyes. "Damn, how you gon' do me like that?" he asked. The hurt in his voice made her cry even harder.

"They not on you. I won't let them wrap you up in this mess," she said and he wanted to believe her but how could he? She had committed the ultimate sin by working with the feds.

Mo Money was torn between killing her now or leaving her alive to put him in jail for the rest of his life. If he killed her now, he feds would surely wrap his black ass up for her murder. He felt like as of now he was living on borrowed time. He shot her one more look that was full of disappointment, tucked his gun and hurried out of the house leaving her crying her eyes out. Once he jumped in his car, he screeched off trying to get as far as he could as quick as he could.

Chapter 16
Risky and B.T

The day that Risky and B.T were due to come home was a sunny October day.

When Mo Money arrived in the back of the building, it looked like Lollapalooza was going on or something. Everybody was out there. Niggas who hadn't been in the hood in years were back there. Women who he hadn't seen since elementary school were out there. The older guys had their families out, grills were going, there was a DJ booth set up and even a big bouncy house for the kids.

He parked his Dodge Charger, tucked his Glock and grabbed the Dior bag he had sitting on his passengers' seat before climbing out of his car. He was dressed in a black Louis Vuitton denim jacket over a black and white Lamie Tee, a pair of jet-black skinny jeans that had rips in the knee and a pair of black Timbs. His long dreads hung freely past his shoulders down to his chest. This was the most uncomfortable he'd felt in a long time. Not knowing what to do, he walked over to where Henno, Wooski D, Pistol, Ray Real and Fool were standing.

"What's the demonstration, beloved?" Henno asked happily extending his hand for a shake.

"What's up, big bro?" he asked returning the smile.

"So, this what it took to get you back in the hood?" Wooski D asked, stepping up to embrace him. Him, Henno and Ray Real were the older Stones from Risky Road. They never got involved in the war between him and Reesie. They were actually the ones advocating for them to squash their beef and bring the hood back together.

"You know for you I'm always only one call away," Mo Money told him. He scanned the parking lot and seen a big dice game going on by where the tennis court used to be. He made his way towards the dice game, passing a few old friends that shot him mean mugs and funny glances.

"What's up, Law?" LB asked him. She was a stud from the hood who he never robbed or shot at so they were still on good terms.

"What's the word, gang? What y'all shooting?"

"Fifties and hundreds," Baby answered, dropping a gang sign with him. Everybody who was older than him was showing him love. They even acted as if they missed him being around. It made him feel missed. After a while a two X pills, his nerves had calmed, and he was actually enjoying himself. Old hoes he used to like that wasn't fucking with him back then, were all in his face now asking for pictures and trying to exchange numbers with him.

When Reesie pulled up with a gang of the shorties, everybody tensed up. People who were just in Mo Money's face were now trying to shy away from him when they saw Reesie heading his way. They all expected something to go down.

"What's up, Solid?" Reesie asked him.

"Shit, what you on, Stone?" he shot back. Reesie smiled showing his gap before extending his hand. They shook up. One thing about them was that even though they hated each other, they respected each other's gangsta fasho. Mo Money noticed how his younger cousin, Molotti was looking at him.

"What's the demo, lil cuz?" He asked.

"What's the demo?" He replied flatly. Him and Mo Money were the same dark skin tone. They had the same full lips with the pink bottom lip, the same dark, beady, sneaky ass eyes. Mo Money was just maybe an inch taller than he was and his dreads were longer. They were what people called identical cousins.

"You good? You don't need shit, do you?"

"Naw, I'm straight, cuz?"

Mo Money could sense that he was making things awkward for his little cousin so he left it at that. Deep down, he was hurt by his reluctance to fuck with him. He noticed that Hot Rod was standing amongst Reesie's crowd glowering at him. Hot Rod always knew how to dress but today something was different about him.

At first, he couldn't place his finger on what it was but then he noticed that it was the jewelry he was wearing. He had on a bussdown Cuban link and a bussdown Rolex. That's when Mo Money looked around and noticed that quite a few people in Reesie's crowd were shining. Reesie, Lil 4, Beezy, Tevo, Bands, Shodyshod and Mylo were all wearing diamond chains and watches. A smile formed on his face. He was taking notes on who he could catch and rob later.

When B.T and Risky pulled up with their mother and sister, you would've thought that it was a few celebrities who had pulled up by how everyone was flocking to get to them. Risky was a slim brown skinned guy with a low cut who stood about 5'9. He was dressed in a Alexander McQueen outfit with a pair of black Alexander McQueen shoes. B.T was lighter than him, like the color of burnt yellow. He had shoulder length dreads, big lips and he stood about 6 feet. He was dressed in a Balenciaga sweatsuit with a pair of Balenciaga runners to match. Both of them wore matching smiles. They knew the hood would be lit for them but they didn't imagine it being to this magnitude. People were recording them and snapping pictures. Reesie stepped up with a handful of bag. He reached in one bag and passed both of the brothers two jewelry boxes apiece. They opened the boxes to reveal thick diamond Cuban link chains with the Double R pendent on them and rose gold presidential Rolexes.

"Welcome home," he told the brothers after embracing both of them with a hug and then a shake. Both Risky and B.T were Four Corner Hustlers.

Mo Money stepped up next. He unzipped his Dior bag and pulled out a big brick of crispy blue face hundreds. He passed one humongous brick to B.T and another to Risky. "Welcome home," he said with a smile showing his big teeth. B.T told everybody that he wanted to take a few pictures with all the original members and they did without hesitation. People who thought they would've never seen Mo Money and Reesie in another picture together were speechless seeing them smile and throw up the 'R' with their hands. They looked like they were never into it.

King Bucky, Cello and Racks pulled up together in Bucky's G63 Benz. They had been watching everybody's Facebook and Instagram pages and when they seen how everybody was posting pictures with Mo Money, they were furious. Niggas were smiling with him like he wasn't one of their biggest opps. When Reesie told them that it was a peace treaty and that nobody was to fuck with him while he was in the hood, Racks knew that he had lost it. The first chance he got to smoke that nigga he was taking it and would deal with the consequences later.

Everybody seemed to gravitate towards B.T and Risky, who were either telling jail stories or reminiscing on the last time they saw whoever it was that they were talking to. Everybody out there was trying hard to impress the brothers with stories of how they were getting money or fucking up the opps.

"Check it out real quick," Risky told Reesie, Mo Money, Baby, Primo and Wooski D. Them along with B.T stepped off to the side where they could talk amongst themselves.

"First things first, its good to finally be back out here with you niggas," he said and everybody nodded in agreement. "It's been a long time and I know a lot of shit done changed but one thing that ain't changed is that everybody right here is from 104th, born and raised in that building." He pointed at the building while glaring at Mo Money. "The shit y'all been having going on with each other ain't right. On the Foe, that's not how we coming and I'm not asking y'all, I'm telling y'all to leave that shit alone," Risky said. His eyes flicking from Mo Money to Reesie trying to read their body language and facial expressions.

This was something he had been waiting to do ever since he heard about their war starting. He was actually mad at the big bros because they didn't step up and squash that shit. A few niggas who he was standing in front of had the say so to do it he was confused as to why they sat back. From what he spent years hearing about both Reesie and Mo Money, he knew that if they were moving as one, Risky Road would be one of the most richest, littest hoods in the city. They were already in the talks.

"On the Foe, we all we got and I fuck with both of y'all so how you think I'ma react if you shoot at him while I'm with him," B.T asked Reesie.

"You know I wouldn't even shoot at him if you was anywhere near him," he replied.

"I'm sure Moe got tints so you wouldn't even know if I was in the car with him or not. What about the shorties that don't even know me? They don't know me to care if I was with him or not," B.T said making it make a lot of sense.

On the Foe, you right," Reesie agreed. "So, y'all want us to just let that shit go and be best friends huh?"

"Just being realistic about the situation, we know that y'all might never be cool again but y'all don't have to like each other to co-exist. I plan on fuckin with both of y'all. Y'all my brothers. I just don't wanna get caught up in the middle of some shit that shouldn't even be going on in the first place," Risky explained. He was closer to Reesie but he loved Mo Money just the same. He looked at both of them as his little brothers.

When Bucky, Racks and Cello walked up, Cello lost it. "On the Four Corner Hustler, I know y'all don't got this hoe ass nigga out here in the mix like everything all well with his bitch ass. He get one day and tomorrow its back up with his hoe ass. Y'all should let me beat his ass one on one real quick," he rasped angrily.

"That shit over with. Moe good," Risky stated.

Cello smacked his lips. "No the fuck he not. Y'all don't know all the snake ass shit this nigga done did over the years. That nigga will never be good back here," he said.

"Shit ain't gone change overnight but we about to slowly but surely get this bitch back in order. The first thing we doing is nipping this shit in the bud as long as Moe claiming Risky Road, he gon be free to move in the hood however he want to."

"Naw, Foe."

"Naw, Foe what?" B.T asked Cello with a frown on his face. Anybody who knew him or even knew of him, knew that he had a short temper and a quick trigger finger. He was a beast with his hands too. Members like Reesie, Mo Money and Racks were known to get active but B.T was the originator. He was the first one stepping on shit and he was anxious to start getting his hands dirty again.

"It ain't gone work like that," Cello said, softening his tone.

"On the Foe, Moe gon' be in the hood with me every fucking day. The first nigga that play with him gon' be the first mufucka I make an example out of," B.T vowed. "Anybody right here got a problem with that, let me know right now," he said challenging everyone right there. Nobody said anything and he felt that power that he was so used to feeling.

"That's what it is then Foe," Reesie spoke up. His lips were pressed together, and his jaws were clinched. He wasn't feeling this shit one bit, but he respected Foe nem too much to argue with them. He knew that nine times out of ten, Risky had a master plan that he was ready to put in motion.

The crowd dispersed and everybody went to enjoying the event that was going on. Bands, who was just starting his rap career, shot a video and even Mo Money got in a few scenes. He hadn't felt this type of love in a long, long time. He had spent the majority of the last decade of his life being a loner. It actually felt good being around his niggas. It felt good being back on the block where it all started at.

Deep down, he missed his hood. He had so many fond memories of being in the building doing all type of bad shit with then men who were surrounding him. Just sitting back observing, he seen that Cello was still the same loud, argumentative ass nigga that he'd always been. Lil 4 was still arrogant and cocky as hell. Racks was still mad at the world and over aggressive as he'd always been. King Bucky still only wanted to get high and crack jokes. Times changed but the niggas he grew up with hadn't changed at all. Everybody grew but nobody changed.

"Aye Moe, I need for you to take me to this hotel. I got a lil bitch there waiting for me," B.T told him. It was after 1AM but the back of the building was still lit.

"Aight," Mo Money replied, leading him to his Charger.

Reesie stood with Hot Rod and Risky filling Risky in on the endeavors he had going on. Risky had already let him know that he was trying to run his bag up. He was the first one out of their crowd to earn a name as a hustler. He inspired the lil bros to hustle the same way B.T inspired the steppers to step. Hot Rod being the stand up nigga that he was decided to hit Risky with a brick of coke just off the strength.

"Yoooo," Hot Rod answered a Facetime from Powder. He had been real distant from him lately but they still spoke from time to time.

"What you on, broski?" Powder asked and he flipped the camera to show him how lit the back of the building was.

"Damn its bussing back, there. What the fuck going on?"

"Two of they homies just got out and they did it big for them," he was saying when Powder's face dropped like he had seen a ghost. Hot Rod turned around to see Racks, Cello and another one of the Foes taking a picture with the Avengers mask that they had on the other day.

"Who is that with that Iron man mask?" Powder asked.

"I think that's the hoe ass nigga, Racks. Why?"

"Because the day the trap got hit, remember I told you that somebody wearing an Iron Man mask got on the phone when JB facetimed me?" Powder asked and he instantly recollected what he was talking about.

"Aye Reesie, let me holla at you," Hot Rod said before pulling him to the side.

***

"So, what the fuck you been doing out here hustling?" B.T asked Mo Money, looking through the dark tinted windows enjoying the scenery as Mo Money drove through the city.

"Man, Foe, all I do is hit licks. I used to fuck with the work but some shit happened and mufuckas scared to do business with me now. I just hit licks and lately I been clapping mufuckas for bread," he admitted. B.T was the one friend that he always idolized. He was the toughest, most gangsta nigga in the hood. When they were shorties, nobody wanted smoke with him and if he caught anybody trying to pull it with any one of the guys, he would get right on their ass. He was a protector and a standup guy all the way around.

"Who all we into it with?"

"Same mufuckas we always been into it with. The Foes off 107th. We into it with damn near everybody from the burbs and we made a few more opps because we was locked in with D Block and Moe nem into it with everybody."

"What's up with D Block nem now?"

"I'm into it with Nut and Binky. Everybody else cool. They still fuckin mufuckas up and getting money."

"You into it with yo' cousin Nut?" B.T asked and Mo Money nodded. "What's up with Diesel nem?"

"Smack and Diesel got check and Bone, that's another story," Mo Money said not wanting to go into detail on what was up with Bone. "I really be on the whole city ass by myself. Mufuckas know what time it is with me. I want smoke with the city," he boasted.

"On the Foe, I was hearing yo' name a lot while I was in that bitch. Niggas was steady talking about how you either robbed or killed somebody they knew."

"Once upon a time, I was checking a real bag but T Stone did some off the wall ass shit and the plug kidnapped my daughter. It's all type of crazy shit that been going on out here. I'ma put you in tune with everything doe," Mo Money told him while peeking at his rearview.

B.T was fresh home so he didn't know the severity of being on point watching them mirrors while you were in traffic. It got quiet for a few seconds.

"What you on now that you out?" he asked B.T.

"Shit, I'm tryna get in my bag but you know I'm not the type to be out here selling drugs. You say you been clapping mufuckas for bread, right? I'm tryna get involved in that."

"Say less," Mo Money replied with a wicked smile.

***

Racks pulled out of the gas station on 103rd after serving a nigga a pound of exotic. He wanted to go back to the back of the building but it was getting late, so he decided to take it in. He was high off pills and tipsy so he figured he might as well go home and invite a bop over.

When he was passing London Town on 101st and Cottage Grove, he saw Reesie's Benz speeding his way. Reesie flashed his brights at him and he pulled over by Jay's Potato

Chip Factory. Reesie's Benz pulled next to his car and Hot Rod jumped out of the passenger's seat. The first thing Racks saw was the fire in his red eyes. The next thing, he saw was the fire leaping from the barrel of Hot Rod's Glock. He couldn't do anything but ball up while Hot rod filled his body with lead. Racks was dead before Hot Rod's stick emptied but Hot Rod kept shooting until his gun clicked. He then hopped back in the passenger's seat of the Benz and the driver sped off.

***

Ever since Mo Money had exposed Ashley for being a rat, she had been trying to reach him to no avail. He didn't want anything to do with her. She thought he was neglecting her out of anger but he was really avoiding her trying to save her from what he felt he needed to do to ensure his freedom. If she wasn't fully cooperating now, then she would be soon or at least that's how he felt. The thing was that he loved her and no matter how hurt he was, he couldn't find it in himself to kill her or have her killed. Ashley really needed to get a hold of him to let him know that she was pregnant.

Her last doctor's appointment revealed that she was seven weeks pregnant. She knew how badly he always wanted a baby by her so she figured that once he heard the news, he would forget about all of the other shit she had going on. She decided to text him to let him know the good news. Seconds later, he texted back telling her to come over.

Ashley drove to Mo Moneys house happily. She knew that her being pregnant would fix everything. Her next step was to convince him to marry her because if they were married, she wouldn't have to testify against him if it ever got to that point. She was so focused on him that she didn't even know that she was getting followed by the Feds. She made it to his house and walked to the front door with a big ass Kool-Aid smile on her face. She rang the doorbell and when it swung open, she was met by the barrel of a small 9mm held by Deja. Deja squeezed the trigger and the first shot hit her in her upper chest spinning her around. The second shot hit her in her face, knocking her to the ground. The two federal agents that were trailing her called in for back up and jumped out their car with their guns drawn.

"Drop the weapon!" The bald head agent yelled at Deja aiming his Sig at her head. She froze in fear and dropped her weapon. The agents rushed her and threw her to the ground next to Ashley who was choking on her own blood. Mo Money had left his phone at home and Ashley was texting her the whole time, instead of him. Deja felt like by Ashley being pregnant that would fuck up everything she had just worked so hard to make right with her man. Ashley was in her way and the only way to solve the problem was to take her out of the equation. She told Mo money that she was going to kill that bitch. He probably thought that she was just talking.

She heard the tires of more Feds pulling up to the scene and that's when she thought about the drugs, guns and bank money that Mo Money had in the house. As the agents pulled her up from the ground, she saw a black SRT Dodge Charger riding by. She knew that Mo Money was looking at her through the dark tinted windows, so she mouthed the words *I love you* to him as the agents guided her to their car.

**Lock Down Publications and Ca$h Presents
Assisted Publishing Packages**

BASIC PACKAGE	**UPGRADED PACKAGE**
$499	$800
Editing	Typing
Cover Design	Editing
Formatting	Cover Design
	Formatting
ADVANCE PACKAGE	**LDP SUPREME PACKAGE**
$1,200	$1,500
Typing	Typing
Editing	Editing
Cover Design	Cover Design
Formatting	Formatting
Copyright registration	Copyright registration
Proofreading	Proofreading
Upload book to Amazon	Set up Amazon account
	Upload book to Amazon
	Advertise on LDP, Amazon and
	Facebook Page

***Other services available upon request.
Additional charges may apply

Lock Down Publications
P.O. Box 944
Stockbridge, GA 30281-9998
Phone: 470 303-9761

Submission Guideline

Submit the first three chapters of your completed manuscript to ldpsubmissions@gmail.com. In the subject line add **Your Book's Title**. The manuscript must be in a Word Doc file and sent as an attachment. Document should be in Times New Roman, double spaced, and in size 12 font. Also, provide your synopsis and full contact information. If sending multiple submissions, they must each be in a separate email.

Have a story but no way to send it electronically? You can still submit to LDP/Ca$h Presents. Send in the first three chapters, written or typed, of your completed manuscript to:

LDP: Submissions Dept
P.O. Box 944
Stockbridge, GA 30281-9998

DO NOT send original manuscript. Must be a duplicate. Provide your synopsis and a cover letter containing your full contact information.

Thanks for considering LDP and Ca$h Presents.

NEW RELEASES

BLOODLINE OF A SAVAGE 1&2
THESE VICIOUS STREETS 1&2
RELENTLESS GOON
RELENTLESS GOON 2
BY PRINCE A. TAUHID

THE BUTTERFLY MAFIA 1-3
BY FUMIYA PAYNE

A THUG'S STREET PRINCESS 1&2
BY MEESHA

CITY OF SMOKE 2
BY MOLOTTI

STEPPERS 1,2&3
THE REAL BADDIES OF CHI-RAQ
BY KING RIO

THE LANE 1&2
BY KEN-KEN SPENCE

THUG OF SPADES 1&2
LOVE IN THE TRENCHES 2
CORNER BOYS
BY COREY ROBINSON

TIL DEATH 3
BY ARYANNA

THE BIRTH OF A GANGSTER 4
BY DELMONT PLAYER

PRODUCT OF THE STREETS 1&2
BY DEMOND "MONEY" ANDERSON

NO TIME FOR ERROR
BY KEESE

MONEY HUNGRY DEMONS
BY TRANAY ADAMS

Coming Soon from Lock Down Publications/Ca$h Presents

IF YOU CROSS ME ONCE 6
ANGEL V
By Anthony Fields

IMMA DIE BOUT MINE 5
By Aryanna

A THUGS STREET PRINCESS 3
By Meesha

PRODUCT OF THE STREETS 3
By Demond Money Anderson

CORNER BOYS 2
By Corey Robinson

THE MURDER QUEENS 6&7
By Michael Gallon

CITY OF SMOKE 3
By Molotti

CONFESSIONS OF A DOPE BOY
By Nicholas Lock

THA TAKEOVER
By Keith Chandler

BETRAYAL OF A G 2
By Ray Vinci

CRIME BOSS
By Playa Ray

Available Now

RESTRAINING ORDER 1 & 2
By **CA$H & Coffee**

LOVE KNOWS NO BOUNDARIES 1-3
By **Coffee**

RAISED AS A GOON I, II, III & IV
BRED BY THE SLUMS I, II, III
BLAST FOR ME I & II
ROTTEN TO THE CORE I II III
A BRONX TALE I, II, III
DUFFLE BAG CARTEL I II III IV V VI
HEARTLESS GOON I II III IV V
A SAVAGE DOPEBOY I II
DRUG LORDS I II III
CUTTHROAT MAFIA I II
KING OF THE TRENCHES
By **Ghost**

LAY IT DOWN I & II
LAST OF A DYING BREED I II
BLOOD STAINS OF A SHOTTA I & II III
By **Jamaica**

LOYAL TO THE GAME I II III
LIFE OF SIN I, II III
By **TJ & Jelissa**

IF LOVING HIM IS WRONG…I & II
LOVE ME EVEN WHEN IT HURTS I II III
By **Jelissa**

PUSH IT TO THE LIMIT
By **Bre' Hayes**

BLOODY COMMAS I & II
SKI MASK CARTEL I, II & III
KING OF NEW YORK I II, III IV V
RISE TO POWER I II III
COKE KINGS I II III IV V
BORN HEARTLESS I II III IV
KING OF THE TRAP I II
By **T.J. Edwards**

WHEN THE STREETS CLAP BACK I & II III
THE HEART OF A SAVAGE I II III IV
MONEY MAFIA I II
LOYAL TO THE SOIL I II III
By **Jibril Williams**

A DISTINGUISHED THUG STOLE MY HEART I II & III
LOVE SHOULDN'T HURT I II III IV
RENEGADE BOYS 1-4
PAID IN KARMA 1-3
SAVAGE STORMS 1-3
AN UNFORESEEN LOVE 1-3
BABY, I'M WINTERTIME COLD 1-3
A THUG'S STREET PRINCESS 1&2
By **Meesha**

A GANGSTER'S CODE 1-3
A GANGSTER'S SYN 1-3
THE SAVAGE LIFE 1-3
CHAINED TO THE STREETS 1-3
BLOOD ON THE MONEY 1-3
A GANGSTA'S PAIN 1-3
BEAUTIFUL LIES AND UGLY TRUTHS
CHURCH IN THESE STREETS
By **J-Blunt**

CUM FOR ME 1-8
An LDP Erotica Collaboration

BLOOD OF A BOSS 1-5
SHADOWS OF THE GAME
TRAP BASTARD
By **Askari**

THE STREETS BLEED MURDER 1-3
THE HEART OF A GANGSTA 1-3
By **Jerry Jackson**

WHEN A GOOD GIRL GOES BAD
By **Adrienne**

THE COST OF LOYALTY 1-3
By **Kweli**

BRIDE OF A HUSTLA 1-3
THE FETTI GIRLS 1-3
CORRUPTED BY A GANGSTA 1-4
BLINDED BY HIS LOVE
THE PRICE YOU PAY FOR LOVE 1-3
DOPE GIRL MAGIC 1-3
By **Destiny Skai**

A KINGPIN'S AMBITION
A KINGPIN'S AMBITION II
I MURDER FOR THE DOUGH
By **Ambitious**

TRUE SAVAGE 1-7
DOPE BOY MAGIC 1-3
MIDNIGHT CARTEL 1-3
CITY OF KINGZ 1&2
NIGHTMARE ON SILENT AVE
THE PLUG OF LIL MEXICO 1&2
CLASSIC CITY
By **Chris Green**

A GANGSTER'S REVENGE 1-4
THE BOSS MAN'S DAUGHTERS 1-5
A SAVAGE LOVE 1&2
BAE BELONGS TO ME 1&2
A HUSTLER'S DECEIT 1-3
WHAT BAD BITCHES DO 1-3
SOUL OF A MONSTER 1-3
KILL ZONE
A DOPE BOY'S QUEEN 1-3
TIL DEATH 1-3
IMMA DIE BOUT MINE 1-4
By **Aryanna**

A DOPEBOY'S PRAYER
By **Eddie "Wolf" Lee**

THE KING CARTEL 1-3
By **Frank Gresham**

THESE NIGGAS AIN'T LOYAL 1-3
By **Nikki Tee**

GANGSTA SHYT 1-3
By **CATO**

THE ULTIMATE BETRAYAL
By **Phoenix**

BOSS'N UP 1-3
By **Royal Nicole**

I LOVE YOU TO DEATH
By **Destiny J**

I RIDE FOR MY HITTA
I STILL RIDE FOR MY HITTA
By **Misty Holt**

LOVE & CHASIN' PAPER
By **Qay Crockett**

TO DIE IN VAIN
SINS OF A HUSTLA
By **ASAD**

BROOKLYN HUSTLAZ
By **Boogsy Morina**

BROOKLYN ON LOCK 1 & 2
By **Sonovia**

GANGSTA CITY
By **Teddy Duke**

A DRUG KING AND HIS DIAMOND 1-3
A DOPEMAN'S RICHES
HER MAN, MINE'S TOO 1&2
CASH MONEY HO'S
THE WIFEY I USED TO BE 1&2
PRETTY GIRLS DO NASTY THINGS
By **Nicole Goosby**

LIPSTICK KILLAH 1-3
CRIME OF PASSION 1-3
FRIEND OR FOE 1-3
By **Mimi**

TRAPHOUSE KING 1-3
KINGPIN KILLAZ 1-3
STREET KINGS 1&2
PAID IN BLOOD 1&2
CARTEL KILLAZ 1-3
DOPE GODS 1&2
By **Hood Rich**

THE STREETS ARE CALLING
By **Duquie Wilson**

STEADY MOBBN' 1-3
THE STREETS STAINED MY SOUL 1-3
By **Marcellus Allen**

WHO SHOT YA 1-3
SON OF A DOPE FIEND 1-4
HEAVEN GOT A GHETTO 1&2
SKI MASK MONEY 1&2
By **Renta**

GORILLAZ IN THE BAY 1-4
TEARS OF A GANGSTA 1/&2
3X KRAZY 1&2
STRAIGHT BEAST MODE 1&2
By **DE'KARI**

TRIGGADALE 1-3
MURDA WAS THE CASE 1-3
By **Elijah R. Freeman**

SLAUGHTER GANG 1-3
RUTHLESS HEART 1-3
By **Willie Slaughter**

GOD BLESS THE TRAPPERS 1-3
THESE SCANDALOUS STREETS 1-3
FEAR MY GANGSTA 1-5
THESE STREETS DON'T LOVE NOBODY 1-2
BURY ME A G 1-5
A GANGSTA'S EMPIRE 1-4
THE DOPEMAN'S BODYGAURD 1&2
THE REALEST KILLAZ 1-3
THE LAST OF THE OGS 1-3
By **Tranay Adams**

MARRIED TO A BOSS 1-3
By **Destiny Skai & Chris Green**

KINGZ OF THE GAME 1-7
CRIME BOSS 1-3
By **Playa Ray**

FUK SHYT
By **Blakk Diamond**

DON'T F#CK WITH MY HEART 1&2
By **Linnea**

ADDICTED TO THE DRAMA 1-3
IN THE ARM OF HIS BOSS
By **Jamila**

LOYALTY AIN'T PROMISED 1&2
By **Keith Williams**

YAYO 1-4
A SHOOTER'S AMBITION 1&2
BRED IN THE GAME
By **S. Allen**

TRAP GOD 1-3
RICH $AVAGE 1-3
MONEY IN THE GRAVE 1-3
CARTEL MONEY
By **Martell Troublesome Bolden**

FOREVER GANGSTA 1&2
GLOCKS ON SATIN SHEETS 1&2
By **Adrian Dulan**

TOE TAGZ 1-4
LEVELS TO THIS SHYT 1&2
IT'S JUST ME AND YOU
By **Ah'Million**

CITY OF SMOKE 3 | MOLOTTI

KINGPIN DREAMS 1-3
RAN OFF ON DA PLUG
By **Paper Boi Rari**

THE STREETS MADE ME 1-3
By **Larry D. Wright**

CONFESSIONS OF A GANGSTA 1-4
CONFESSIONS OF A JACKBOY 1-3
CONFESSIONS OF A HITMAN
By **Nicholas Lock**

I'M NOTHING WITHOUT HIS LOVE
SINS OF A THUG
TO THE THUG I LOVED BEFORE
A GANGSTA SAVED XMAS
IN A HUSTLER I TRUST
By **Monet Dragun**

QUIET MONEY 1-3
THUG LIFE 1-3
EXTENDED CLIP 1&2
A GANGSTA'S PARADISE
By **Trai'Quan**

CAUGHT UP IN THE LIFE 1-3
THE STREETS NEVER LET GO 1-3
By **Robert Baptiste**

NEW TO THE GAME 1-3
MONEY, MURDER & MEMORIES 1-3
By **Malik D. Rice**

CREAM 2-3
THE STREETS WILL TALK
By **Yolanda Moore**

THE STREETS WILL NEVER CLOSE 1-3
By **K'ajji**

LIFE OF A SAVAGE 1-4
A GANGSTA'S QUR'AN 1-4
MURDA SEASON 1-3
GANGLAND CARTEL 1-3
CHI'RAQ GANGSTAS 1-4
KILLERS ON ELM STREET 1-3
JACK BOYZ N DA BRONX 1-3
A DOPEBOY'S DREAM 1-3
JACK BOYS VS DOPE BOYS 1-3
COKE GIRLZ
COKE BOYS
SOSA GANG 1&2
BRONX SAVAGES
BODYMORE KINGPINS
BLOOD OF A GOON
By **Romell Tukes**

CONCRETE KILLA 1-3
VICIOUS LOYALTY 1-3
By **Kingpen**

THE ULTIMATE SACRIFICE 1-6
KHADIFI
IF YOU CROSS ME ONCE 1-3
ANGEL 1-4
IN THE BLINK OF AN EYE
By **Anthony Fields**

THE LIFE OF A HOOD STAR
By **Ca$h & Rashia Wilson**

NIGHTMARES OF A HUSTLA 1-3
BLOOD AND GAMES 1&2
By **King Dream**

GHOST MOB
By **Stilloan Robinson**

HARD AND RUTHLESS 1&2
MOB TOWN 251
THE BILLIONAIRE BENTLEYS 1-3
REAL G'S MOVE IN SILENCE
By **Von Diesel**

MOB TIES 1-7
SOUL OF A HUSTLER, HEART OF A KILLER 1-3
GORILLAZ IN THE TRENCHES
By **SayNoMore**

BODYMORE MURDERLAND 1-3
THE BIRTH OF A GANGSTER 1-4
By **Delmont Player**

FOR THE LOVE OF A BOSS 1&2
By **C. D. Blue**

KILLA KOUNTY 1-5
By **Khufu**

MOBBED UP 1-4
THE BRICK MAN 1-5
THE COCAINE PRINCESS 1-10
STEPPERS 1-3
SUPER GREMLIN 1-4
By **King Rio**

MONEY GAME 1&2
By **Smoove Dolla**

A GANGSTA'S KARMA 1-4
By **FLAME**

KING OF THE TRENCHES 1-3
By **GHOST & TRANAY ADAMS**

CITY OF SMOKE 3 | MOLOTTI

QUEEN OF THE ZOO 1&2
By **Black Migo**

GRIMEY WAYS 1-3
BETRAYAL OF A G
By **Ray Vinci**

XMAS WITH AN ATL SHOOTER
By **Ca$h & Destiny Skai**

KING KILLA 1&2
By **Vincent "Vitto" Holloway**

BETRAYAL OF A THUG 1&2
By **Fre$h**

THE MURDER QUEENS 1-5
By **Michael Gallon**

FOR THE LOVE OF BLOOD 1-4
By **Jamel Mitchell**

HOOD CONSIGLIERE 1&2
NO TIME FOR ERROR
By **Keese**

PROTÉGÉ OF A LEGEND 1&2
LOVE IN THE TRENCHES 1&2
By **Corey Robinson**

THE PLUG'S RUTHLESS DAUGHTER
By **Tony Daniels**

BORN IN THE GRAVE 1-3
CRIME PAYS
By **Self Made Tay**

MOAN IN MY MOUTH
By **XTASY**

TORN BETWEEN A GANGSTER AND A GENTLEMAN
By **J-BLUNT & Miss Kim**

LOYALTY IS EVERYTHING 1-3
CITY OF SMOKE 1&2
By **Molotti**

HERE TODAY GONE TOMORROW 1&2
By **Fly Rock**

WOMEN LIE MEN LIE 1-4
FIFTY SHADES OF SNOW 1-3
STACK BEFORE YOU SPLURGE
GIRLS FALL LIKE DOMINOES
NAÏVE TO THE STREETS
By **ROY MILLIGAN**

PILLOW PRINCESS
By **S. Hawkins**

THE BUTTERFLY MAFIA 1-3
SALUTE MY SAVAGERY 1&2
By **Fumiya Payne**

THE LANE 1&2
By Ken-Ken Spence

THE PUSSY TRAP 1-5
By **Nene Capri**

DIRTY DNA
By **Blaque**

SANCTIFIED AND HORNY
by **XTASY**

BOOKS BY LDP'S CEO, CA$H

TRUST IN NO MAN
TRUST IN NO MAN 2
TRUST IN NO MAN 3
BONDED BY BLOOD
SHORTY GOT A THUG
THUGS CRY
THUGS CRY 2
THUGS CRY 3
TRUST NO BITCH
TRUST NO BITCH 2
TRUST NO BITCH 3
TIL MY CASKET DROPS
RESTRAINING ORDER
RESTRAINING ORDER 2
IN LOVE WITH A CONVICT
LIFE OF A HOOD STAR
XMAS WITH AN ATL SHOOTER